Sean turned her to face

He raised her head with his fingertips to her chin.

Their eyes locked.

She's so beautiful.

That same unseen chemistry surrounded them. It was intense and undeniable.

"This got us into our situation the last time. Remember?" she asked, even as her eyes dipped for a moment to his mouth.

Memories of kissing her made him clear his throat and take a step back before he gave in to the temptation to pull her close and do just that. Again. And again.

"Right," he agreed.

Montgomery released a long breath and touched her fingertips to her lips as she turned away as well. "Focus on today. We'll deal with anything else tomorrow," she said, her voice back to authoritative. "Remember everything we went over and stick to the script. Just add—"

"Charm," Sean interjected with his winning smile.

* * *

The Pregnancy Proposal by Niobia Bryant
is part of the Cress Brothers series.

Dear Reader,

I am excited to present *The Pregnancy Proposal*, book four in the Cress Brothers series. Hopefully, you'll find Sean and Montgomery's romance just as "sexy, funny and oh so real" as Gabriel and Monica's, Coleman and Jillian's, and Lincoln and Bobbie's. I loved writing the story of one night of passion blooming into a sensual romance and amazing love story—complete with a baby on the way!

Sean and Montgomery were made for each other, but these two have some challenges to overcome on their road to happily-ever-after. I enjoyed every moment of the ride with sighs at the drama, smiles at the romance, tears at the heartache and some blushing at the steamy parts...

As always, I encourage you to create the reading zone of your choice—whether in print or in an ebook. Take this time for yourself to get into this book that hopefully reminds you of your love story or inspires you to go after a romance adventure of your own.

Love truly is grand.

Best,

N.

NIOBIA BRYANT

——

THE PREGNANCY PROPOSAL

Recycling programs
for this product may
not exist in your area.

ISBN-13: 978-1-335-58142-6

The Pregnancy Proposal

Copyright © 2022 by Niobia Bryant

For questions and comments about the quality of this book, please contact us at CustomerService@Harlequin.com.

Harlequin Enterprises ULC
22 Adelaide St. West, 41st Floor
Toronto, Ontario M5H 4E3, Canada
www.Harlequin.com

Printed in U.S.A.

Niobia Bryant is the award-winning and nationally bestselling author of fifty romance and mainstream commercial fiction works. Twice she has won the RT Reviewers' Choice Best Book Award for African American/Multicultural Romance. Her books have appeared in *Ebony*, *Essence*, the *New York Post*, the *Star-Ledger*, the *Dallas Morning News* and many other national publications. One of her bestselling books was adapted to film.

Books by Niobia Bryant

Harlequin Desire

Cress Brothers

One Night with Cinderella
The Rebel Heir
An Offer from Mr. Wrong
The Pregnancy Proposal

Harlequin Kimani

A Billionaire Affair
Tempting the Billionaire

Visit the Author Profile page at Harlequin.com, or niobiabryant.net, for more titles.

You can also find Niobia Bryant on Facebook, along with other Harlequin Desire authors, at Facebook.com/harlequindesireauthors!

As always, this one is dedicated to the wonderful thing called love.

One

Sean Cress looked out the window at the streets of Manhattan, New York, from his seat in the rear of a blacked-out luxury SUV. His thoughts were full and he barely noticed the traffic, the New Yorkers walking the streets at a fast pace, or the towering buildings that were either sleek and modern or of stately classical architecture. He was too busy wishing he were headed to the set of one of his numerous cooking shows. As a chef, the merging of his talent in cooking and his innate charm as an on-air personality had created television and streaming gold. Twice he had been named one of *People* magazine's Sexiest Chefs Alive. His extravagant, fast-paced celebrity lifestyle of A-list events added to his allure. He knew that and used every bit of it to his advantage, enjoying the lime-light and the ladies.

And he was confident that same popularity and acclaim would secure him the position as Chief Executive Officer of his family's powerful culinary empire. His parents, Phillip Cress Senior and Nicolette Lavoie-Cress, had formed Cress, INC. after successful careers as chefs with established restaurants, more than two dozen bestselling cookbooks and guides and countless prestigious awards. Their corporation included nationally syndicated cooking shows, cookware, online magazines, an accredited cooking school and a nonprofit foundation. Food was their life and they passed that passion on to their children.

Sean and his brothers all held executive positions in the company and were acclaimed chefs themselves. Lincoln, his father's newly discovered heir born to him in England before his marriage to Nicolette, had been welcomed into the fold as the President of Sustainability. Phillip Junior ran the Cress Family Foundation. Gabriel led up the restaurant division, Coleman oversaw the online magazines and websites and Lucas supervised the cookware line. Sean's duty was the syndicated cooking shows, including those in which he starred.

Their father, Phillip Senior, dangled the succession of one of them to the Cress, INC. throne, pitting them against each other in the past few years—even though they were raised to be loyal and loving to one another. Each had wanted to make their autocratic father proud and steer the already juggernaut company into a bigger and brighter future. But in time, as their father never actually stepped down and several of the brothers made it clear they no longer wanted to be the CEO, the siblings had regained their closeness.

Even if Lincoln, Gabriel and Coleman no longer wanted the position, Sean did.

With the revelation of their father's heart condition and then his subsequent cardiac surgery just a week ago, it was clear their patriarch would not be able to continue the daily grind of managing a massive company. Phillip Junior, Lucas and he were still in the running for the coveted spot. And Sean had big plans for the company by diversifying into owning a food channel to stream their cooking shows instead of having them played on other networks. He felt the success of his division and his popularity and stardom made him the face of the brand and the clear heir apparent. He just *knew* the position was his.

Until this damn scandal.

Sean pinched the bridge of his nose and cleared his throat. Of late, scandal and the Cress family seemed to go hand in hand. First with Monica, their former housekeeper, becoming Gabriel's wife and heir to a massive fortune left behind by her father—an A-list movie actor she never knew. Then the family—and the press—learning that their father had an illegitimate heir back in England conceived just before he left the country to attend college in Paris. The very last thing the family needed was one of Sean's former bedmates releasing a steamy sex tape of him.

He clenched his jaw, remembering the reaction of his mother who loved her family, her cooking and her privacy—and not always in that order.

If not for the scandal ruining the Cress, INC. brand and hurting his position within the company, Sean couldn't care less about the video. It was years old. The woman had been long forgotten. And sex was a natural thing. Besides, the revelation of just how "equipped" he was had increased his popularity— particularly with the ladies.

His family, of course, cared nothing about the upside of the salacious situation.

So far they had kept the news of the video from Phillip Senior who would undoubtedly be so riled up as to cause a physical setback. Lessening the effect of the drama was essential for his father's health, his mother's sanity and his position within Cress, INC.

He'd hired one of the best in the public relations game to get the job done.

Sean looked over at Montgomery Morgan sitting on the opposite end of the leather rear seat of the SUV. The top-notch publicist was talking low on her phone as she used a stylus to write notes on her iPad before she tucked her bone-straight black hair behind her ear.

"We'll be pulling up any minute," Montgomery said, her voice crisp and clear.

He continued eyeing her and enjoyed himself because the woman looked phenomenal. Jet-black hair brought out the sepia hues in her medium brown complexion. High cheekbones and a slightly square chin were complemented by her full toothy smile, dimples and beautiful feline-like eyes with long lashes. As much as she was a beauty, Montgomery Morgan was also intelligent, levelheaded, cool, reserved and professional. Very straitlaced. In control.

Until she's not.

Two months ago, while attending a dinner party thrown by his brother Gabriel, and her friend/client Monica, he and Montgomery had gotten stuck in the elevator of the couple's luxury townhouse. As the minutes ticked by while they were trapped alone in the confined space, the unflappable publicist had been anything but calm.

Montgomery glanced over and caught his eyes on her. He didn't shift his gaze; instead, he enjoyed the full sight of her face. Her eyes locked with his and her lashes fluttered before she lightly bit her bottom lip.

In that moment he knew that like him, she remembered just what had happened between them on that elevator. Memories of their cries of passion replayed for him. It had been an hour or better of wild abandon before the elevator light came on and exposed their nudity as they rushed into their clothing and agreed it would never happen again.

Best sex ever.

"Hold on one sec," she said before lowering her phone to press the button for another call as she looked away from him. "Montgomery Morgan."

Sean bit back a smile at her formal businesslike tone. Ever the professional.

"What?" Montgomery snapped, sitting up straighter in the seat.

His driver, Colin, slowed the SUV to a stop in front of a midtown Manhattan hotel. Awaiting them was a crowd of onlookers and paparazzi. Sean was more used to the fanfare than the rest of his family, although they were all well-known in their own right.

He shifted his gaze back to Montgomery as her jaw clenched and she closed her eyes with a slight shake of her head. "Something wrong?" he asked.

All of the possible emergent situations ran through his mind. An accident? Medical emergency? Death?

He felt concern for the normally stoic woman.

Before their one-night liaison, he and Montgomery had only been cordial when in each other's company at events thrown by Monica and Gabriel. He'd only contacted her last week after the release of the sex tape. Although Cress, INC. had their own publicity and marketing staff, he had wanted Montgomery's expertise in dealing with high-profile clients and had been relieved when she agreed to represent him.

"Montgomery," he said, reaching to touch her wrist when her head lowered.

She stiffened for a moment and then looked over at him. "I'm pregnant," she revealed in a harsh whisper before swiftly turning and opening the door to exit the vehicle.

Sean felt gut punched. "What?" he snapped.

Out the window he watched as she took a deep breath, straightened the Italian cashmere camel trench she wore over a tailored cream pantsuit and slid on oversize shades before walking to come around the rear of the vehicle. And just like that, her facade was back in place, even though she left him completely rattled.

Pregnant?

By me?

His heart pounded.

Knock-knock.

He looked over to his right to find Montgomery had tapped her knuckles against the window. Colin now stood beside her, keeping the crowd back from the vehicle. They awaited his signal that he was ready.

I'm not.

But he took his own steadying breath, slid on his black aviator shades and pulled the latch on the door. Colin pulled it open wide and Sean climbed out, instantly surrounded by the yells of the crowd as he slid his hands into the pockets of the dark gray coat he wore over matching sweater and wool slacks.

"Sean!"

"We love you, Sean!"

"Are you still with the woman in the tape?"

"Sexy Sean!"

"Any statement on the scandal and the effect on Cress, INC.?"

"I saw the tape!"

"We all did!"

Remembering Montgomery's advice, Sean kept his face unreadable as they made their way across the sidewalk into the five-star hotel where she'd set up a press junket. Her strategy was to address the scandal fully, answer all questions and then move on from it. Hopefully.

They entered the building and swiftly moved across the beautifully adorned lobby with its towering gilded ceilings. Aware of the eyes still on them, Sean fought to maintain his composure even as he felt he might just be losing his mind.

A child?

"Are you pregnant by me?" he asked as soon as they turned the corner toward the gilded elevators.

Montgomery faced him. Even with his over six-foot height, her five foot eight inches and heels brought them nearly eye level. "*If* I'm pregnant, yes it would be yours but let's talk about this later," she said before spinning to press the button for the elevator.

Sean shifted to stand in front of her. "You're just going to drop a bomb on me like that?" he asked, not hiding his exasperation. "And right before a round of interviews, Montgomery?"

She nodded and began to pace. "You're right. It just kind of came out. I was shocked, Sean. I apologize. It's just this morning at my office, my assistant kept nagging me to take a pregnancy test and I finally did it just to shut her up," she said before massaging her temples. "I took the test and left to meet up with you. She called with the results and it shocked me. I honestly did not think I was pregnant."

"Why did she think you were pregnant?" he asked, voicing his curiosity.

"Moody. Sleepy. Hungry. Constantly," she stressed.

"And your cycle?" he asked after hesitating a moment to do so, knowing it was personal.

Montgomery looked affronted. "Really?"

"Considering the situation?" he asked while holding up his hands. "Absolutely."

"I have a highly stressful job and it's irregular at times," she explained. "Look, I feel it needs to be confirmed by a doctor before we flip and lose our minds. Really, I shouldn't have said anything until I knew for sure."

Sean released a breath.

A baby.

I could be a father?

He wasn't ready.

Sean *loved* his life and the freedom to do whatever he wanted. He didn't want to change a thing about it—and so love and settling down with one woman was not a part of his plan. He could easily see himself as The Forever Bachelor. Wifeless. Childless. Enjoying his freedom. Paternity meant sacrifices he was not willing to make, and that was exactly what it took to be a good parent. Not just a sperm donor or sire, but a fully involved father.

It was nothing to take lightly.

The elevator doors slid open and Montgomery stepped on before he followed behind her.

"Damn," she swore as she kept her gaze down on the tips of her polished leather boots as she fidgeted nervously.

Sean turned her to face him again and raised her head with his fingertips to her chin.

Their eyes locked.

She's so beautiful.

That same unseen chemistry surrounded them. It was intense and undeniable.

"This got us into this situation the last time. Remember?" she asked, even as her eyes dipped for a moment to his mouth.

Memories of kissing her made him clear his throat and take a step back before he gave in to the temptation to pull her close and do just that. Again. And again. "Right," he agreed.

Montgomery released a long breath and touched her fingertips to her lips as she turned away as well. "Focus on today. We'll deal with anything else tomorrow," she said, her voice back to authoritative. "Remember everything we went over and stick to the script. Just add—"

"Charm," Sean interjected with his winning smile.

Montgomery looked up at him with a shake of her head and the hint of a smile. "Exactly," she dryly agreed. "Remember this is not to specifically address the scandal but to show you are not shying away from the press because of it. The major topic is your new cooking show and upcoming cookbook, but someone may try to address it with you—whether directly or in a roundabout way."

"I'm disappointed that more respect wasn't shown for a very personal and private moment," he said, remembering the script she crafted for him that was actually very close to his true sentiments. "In my position it's hard to know what is real and staged. That is my biggest regret."

"Excellent!" Montgomery said with a wink and brief nod meant to encourage.

The elevator doors opened and she led him to the suite with a view of Central Park. Her team had turned the room into a set complete with chairs, backdrop, lighting and a few cameras. "Everyone is here and has been set up in the adjoining suite with refreshments and gift bags of Cress merchandise. Either myself or one of my team will check on you between each interview," she continued. "Ready?"

To be a dad? No.

Although he knew it wasn't what she meant, it was all he could think about.

"Yes," Sean said, moving to take the seat she pointed out to him.

The door opened and a petite woman with short, naturally curly hair entered. Her small face was nearly overwhelmed with large, round spectacles. He opened one of the bottles of water on the small table beside him and filled a glass as he watched Montgomery remove her overcoat. She handed it and her tote to the woman he assumed to be her observant and persistent assistant.

He eyed Montgomery's build that was more slender than thick but with curves. The suit she wore was tailored to fit and stylish.

His eyes dipped to her belly.

If she's pregnant she's close to two months.

The thought of a baby made his gut clench. He'd never even been on a date with Montgomery. Never even shared a full-blown conversation on major topics. Now they were expected to co-parent?

"Sean, this is my executive assistant, Hanna," Montgomery said as they walked over to him.

Sean eyed the woman with a nod. "Nice to meet you," he said.

Hanna gave him a nod as well as an up-and-down look. "In person the man lives up to the myth," she whispered to Montgomery.

Sean heard her clearly and bit back a smile.

Montgomery gave her assistant a hard stare and received a helpless shrug in return. "How's the lighting setup on him?" she asked the cameraman.

"Perfect," the man said after taking a test shot.

"Of course," Montgomery muttered dryly.

Sean did give *her* his best smile.

Montgomery turned but not before he saw her roll her eyes.

He chuckled. Even that was a break from the facade of business-only perfection that Montgomery favored and had made her one of the most sought-after publicists on the East Coast. He was relying on her to clear up the scandal and secure his selection as the new CEO of Cress, INC., making her substantial fee well worth the cost.

And if she's pregnant?

Sean frowned as he turned his head to look out the window at Central Park in the distance.

"Are you okay?"

Sean was puzzled by both the male and female voices asking the question. He shifted his gaze from the window to find the cameraman querying him and Hanna looking at her boss. Montgomery and he looked at each other. In her eyes he saw what he was feeling.

Worry.

They both looked away.

"I'm fine," they said in unison.

It was Hanna's and the cameraman's turn to share an odd look.

Sean took another sip of water as his first interviewer was led into the suite. He adjusted his frame in the club chair and stiffened his spine as he prepared himself to try his best to not let the thought of pending fatherhood ruin his chance at redemption.

* * *

"This was not a part of my plan," Montgomery muttered as she looked down at the pregnancy test now encased in a clear Ziploc bag before she looked up at her reflection in the mirror of the suite's bathroom. "Damn."

I can't be pregnant. I just can't. Not now. Not yet.

Montgomery had wanted to thrive in her business before meeting her Mr. Perfect, fall in love, get married and *then* start a family. After years of success and building a support system with her business, Montgomery had felt ready to find the man for her and maybe in three to five years have a child. She had become fastidious and a bit dogged in finding the man who checked everything on her list of must-haves. She was on numerous dating apps for professionals and frequented places all the women's magazines said were ideal for meeting men like hardware stores, golf courses, cigar lounges, gyms and churches. She went on blind dates. Prayed about it. And stayed on the lookout.

It had become a part-time job or side hustle. Montgomery was on a mission. She *wanted* companionship, love and steamy sex, but finding "the one" wasn't panning out. Outside of work, her friends and family, she was lonesome and afraid she would forever be single.

And now I might be a single mother.

She balled the plastic-covered test into her grip. In just one night she might have changed the trajectory of her life. Just once Montgomery "Ms. Perfect" Morgan had lost total control. Quickly and with plenty of fiery passion that had been undeniable.

More, Sean. Give me more.

Montgomery flushed with warmth at the memory of the words she gasped before he obeyed her wish. Deeply. Every pulse on her body fluttered to life.

Just like that night.

In the reflection her eyes widened before she rushed to shove the baggie into her tote before turning on the faucet and bending to press cool water to her neck. It failed in erasing the heat of her desire for Sean Cress.

The man was trouble. Handsome, charming, sexy and flirtatious, but trouble nonetheless.

As the publicist for The Bridge, Monica's non-profit benefiting children aged out of the foster care system, Montgomery had soon become the woman's friend, making running into Sean Cress at both business and family events inevitable. Over the past two years they had always been polite when crossing each other's path, but there had also been lingering looks, mildly flirty banter and innocent touches that created a spark. Montgomery was well aware that Sean found her attractive, and his smiles let her know that he was fully tuned in to the attraction she had for him. But neither acted on it.

Until they both stepped onto the elevator to ride up a level and somewhere in between the first and second floors, the sounds of metal grinding echoed around them just before the lights flickered...

Montgomery instinctively took a step closer to Sean as her dread kicked into overdrive. "You think you're over your childhood fear of elevators...until you get stuck on one," she dryly said as she began to frantically press the buttons on the control panel.

Sean reached into the inner pocket of his blazer to remove his phone. "I'll call for help," he said, his deep voice echoing in the small space.

Montgomery rested her head against the wall as her normal cool composure began to fade. "Why did I get on this death trap? Why did I get on this death trap? Why did I get on this death trap?" she repeated.

Something pressed to her lower back and she whipped around as her heart pounded. It was Sean's hand and she felt some relief at his presence, knowing she was being irrational but unable to fight back her distress.

"There's no signal," Sean said, looking down at her in concern. "But I'm sure help is on the way."

The lights went off.

Montgomery squealed before she flung herself at Sean's body and wrapped her arms around his neck in panic, squeezing her eyes shut even though darkness reigned. "What if we drop? What if there's a fire? What if—"

"Shhh. It'll be okay," Sean assured her as he wrapped one arm around her body to hold her close. "We'll be okay."

She nodded against his neck, feeling comforted by his strength and the gentle way he rocked their bodies back and forth to calm her as he massaged circles on her lower back. Consoling her. It felt good to rely on someone else. Really good.

Too good.

Montgomery took an extra inhale of his warm cologne. It was enticing.

"Everyone has fears," he said. "I'm sure I'd hit a

pitch higher than an opera singer if a snake crossed my path."

She felt a little less crazy about her outburst and managed a bit of a smile.

"A little light will help," Sean said. "I'll use the flashlight on my phone."

She still clung to him and enjoyed it. Her heart pounded. Her breathing was fast. And her pulse sped. Sean's body felt as hard and defined as it looked in his tailored clothing. She felt heady and overwhelmed by him. And her desire.

It was hard to deny in the close quarters with their bodies pressed together.

"Here we go," he said.

With regret, she leaned back and opened her eyes. The light was cast on their faces. She felt transfixed as her eyes flittered over his square-shaped face. His strong chin, cheekbones and jawline were softened by his mouth and sexy downturned dark eyes with long lashes. He truly was handsome. Beautiful even. With his face clean-shaven and his curly hair cut low, he looked younger than his thirty-seven years.

She eyed his soft and tempting mouth as she bit her lip.

His hold of her tightened a bit.

She looked up and their eyes locked.

Chemistry rose quickly and seemed to radiate from their bodies to bounce off the walls.

She felt breathless at the desire she saw in the brown depths of his sparkling eyes.

This was exciting and like nothing she had ever felt

*before. She nearly ached and trembled from wanting
to feel his mouth on hers. And so much more.*

"Montgomery," he moaned.

It was her undoing

*"Kiss me," she begged, throwing away any and
all inhibitions.*

*And he did with a groan that revealed he was tired
of the torture of not tasting her lips.*

*The first feel of his mouth touching down upon
hers delivered a jolt that was electric.*

*She tilted her head a bit to the side to enjoy it.
Revel in the feel of him and how it made her feel more
alive than ever. His tongue touched hers before he
suckled the tip into his mouth. Her hands playing
with his nape as his strong fingers danced up and
down her spine before he began to undo the zip of
the lemon corseted satin dress she wore.*

She offered no objections.

*And when the dress slid down her body and around
her matching heels, she was too far lost in her want
of him to deny herself the pleasure…*

A sudden knock interrupted her steamy recollec-
tion. With a gasp of surprise Montgomery looked
over at the closed door of the en suite. Even now
the memory of the heated moments they'd shared on
that elevator made her pulse race. She ran her hands
through the length of her hair. "Yeah?" she called.

"You okay, Montgomery?" Sean asked.

Her body instantly betrayed her. Everything worked
a bit harder in reaction to him on the other side of the
door. Her heart. Her pulse points. Her stomach. The
fleshy bud nestled behind the lips of her femininity.

The explosive night they'd shared did absolutely nothing to quench her thirst. In fact, it left her parched.

She plastered on her cool, calm and collected expression before opening the door.

Sean was leaning against the wall with his ankles crossed and his hands deep into the pockets of his topcoat. "You okay?" he asked again.

His eyes dipped to her belly and Montgomery instinctively pressed a palm to it. "I'm good," she said, sliding her tote up onto her arm as she stepped into the foyer to stand before him. "And you did great with the junket today."

"I'm glad it's over and hopefully it will be the end of the scandal," he said.

"Hopefully, no other sex tapes from random hookups will appear," she added as she moved away from him to give the now-empty suite one last walk-through.

"Ouch. Judgmental much?" he asked.

Montgomery opened the door to the bedroom and turned on the light before glancing back over her shoulder at him now standing behind her. "Sorry," she said, not sounding like she meant it, before she entered the bedroom to walk around with a cursory look.

"I am an adult who enjoys sex," Sean said, stepping into the room to lightly touch Montgomery's wrist. "And if my memory serves me, so do you."

She looked up at him, all too aware of the feel of his fingertips against her pulse and his deep brown eyes resting on her face. That same attraction between them sizzled. She felt hungry for him. With a shake of her head to break the spell, she looked away but her eyes landed on the bed. She envisioned Sean and her naked upon it. Enjoying sex with each other.

Stroke by delicious stroke.

Montgomery turned away from the mirage with a tremble, wishing she weren't haunted by their rough cries filling the elevator as they climaxed together.

She caught Sean's eyes resting on the bed as well before he locked his gaze with hers.

There was no denying the intensity in the dark depths. Or the way they made her feel hot and a little light-headed. She eased her wrist from his grip and hurried to rush past him to leave the bedroom. Pressing a hand to her throat she felt her pulse pounding against her palm.

Once the lights had returned and the elevator began to move upward, they had rushed into their clothing and emerged to an awaiting crowd as if nothing had happened between them. In the months following they had never spoken of it or even given the slightest inkling that they had done *things* to each other in that elevator. Naughty things.

Until today.

The pregnancy talk unlocked the door they both had seemed to close.

"Thanks, Montgomery."

She whirled. "For the sex?" she asked, feeling the incredulity on her face.

Sean lowered his head with a chuckle before looking up at her.

The move caused her gut to clench.

Why does this man get to me like this?

"No. Thank you for the work you put in to help

this scandal die down," he explained with a smile—
that smile.

The charming, disarming one.

"It's my job," she said with a succinct nod.

Get it together, Montgomery.

"You're great at it," Sean said. "And the sex."

Montgomery gave him a hard look meant to chas-
tise. "We're not doing that," she said.

Sean looked amused. "Having sex?" he asked.

"Having sex. Talking about having sex. Reminisc-
ing on when we had sex," she said, ticking each off on
a finger. "Doing replays on the sex like it was sport
or ranking it like I was requesting a score. It was sex,
not the Olympics."

Sean bit back a smile.

"Oooh."

They both looked to the door to find it open with
Hanna standing in the foyer with her face a mask of
shock and then excited approval.

Just great.

"I'll be right with you, Hanna," Montgomery said,
rubbing her fingertips over her brows to ease her rising anxiety.

Thankfully, her assistant immediately stepped out
of the room and closed the door behind herself. Still,
Montgomery walked over to the door and opened it
to ensure the little busybody—who was as smart as
she was inquisitive—did not have her ear pressed to
the wood. With a heavy breath she closed the door
and leaned against it, feeling emotional and drained.

"Hey, hey, hey," Sean rushed to say as he strode
over to her. "What's wrong?"

In truth, she needed a hug. A tight one. The kind where she could rest her head on a strong chest and let him offer her the strength she felt lacking.

Like in the elevator.

And look what happened.

Montgomery locked her knees and swallowed down all of her feelings. "I'm okay," she lied, stepping back behind her facade.

Just as she had nearly all her life as she grew up the daughter of a devout minister. Every decision, every action, every reaction, was keeping in mind that she was a preacher's kid. The weight of what was expected had felt heavy, and her father had made those obligations clear.

So how do I tell him I'm unmarried and pregnant?

"I gotta go," Montgomery said, sounding as defeated as she felt and needing to be alone to be as weepy as she wanted. "I'll be in touch about the PR and the—the—the—"

"The pregnancy," Sean provided.

She leveled her eyes on his. "The pregnancy," she repeated. "I'll have it confirmed by my doctor and let you know."

"Okay," he said with his eyes studying her.

It made her entire body tingle.

For a moment, as they stood there looking at each other, surrounded by that now-familiar hum of awareness, she could almost believe that everything would be just fine.

Almost.

Two

One week later

Cloaked by the darkness of night, Sean lay on his back in the middle of his king-size bed, looking up at the tray ceiling with its brocade design. The expansive bedroom suite was quiet with none of the noise of his large family breaking through the thick walls or doors of the five-story Victorian-era townhouse in the prominent Lenox Hill section of Manhattan. The entire family had resided in the Cress family townhouse growing up, and although Gabriel, Coleman and Lincoln lived in their own places across New York, it was still a full house. Currently, his parents' quarters took up the entire third floor. On the fourth and fifth floors were three full bedroom suites, and a large den and pantry. Lucas and Sean lived on the fifth, with Sean having moved upstairs to give Phillip Junior, his wife, Raquel, and their school-aged daughter more space on the fourth. Their housekeeper, Felice, who also lived with them full-time, had a suite of rooms and her own entrance in the cellar. Even with nearly ten thousand square feet, five floors, a cellar and the roof garden, it still felt a little crowded with so many adults living together.

He was thankful for the sound structure because he had a lot on his mind.

Sean looked out the glass wall, flanked by gray suede curtains secured by leather ties, that showcased a view of the night landscape in the distance and the snow-covered limbs of the towering tree in the backyard. The view was peaceful, while his thoughts were troubled.

With awaiting confirmation of Montgomery's pregnancy, the blowback from the sex tape scandal, filming new seasons of two cooking shows, working on recipes for his newest cookbook, fighting for the CEO position of Cress, INC. and maintaining his busy social schedule, Sean felt pulled in all directions.

The possibility of becoming a father outweighed them all.

He thought of Montgomery—beautiful with her cool facade that hid a fiery appetite.

More, Sean. Give me more, she had begged.

And there in the dark elevator with only his phone dropped to the floor offering a stream of light up onto the ceiling, he had obeyed her command as he felt for her leg and eased it up onto his shoulder. Her gasp of pleasure echoed around them and he remembered longing for enough light to see her face. Her beauty. Her passion. Her pleasure.

Sean leaned over to pick up his phone from the nightstand. He felt the urge to call Montgomery.

And say what?

That he just wanted to hear her voice and check on her, knowing she was worried.

With a wry chuckle, Sean used his free hand to fling back the woven coverlet that matched the decor of all shades of gray from light to charcoal. He sat up nude on the side of the bed, thankful for the silk woven rug on the floor under the massive bed to shield his feet from the cold hardwood floors. Leaving his phone atop the crisp white cotton sheets before rising, he made his way over to his en suite to retrieve his black terry-cloth robe embroidered with his initials in white letters. Barefoot, he left his suite. He stopped halfway across the dimly lit den that centered the entire floor with the suites on one side, and the pantry, wrought iron staircase and elevator on the other. He slid his hands into the pockets of his robe and looked out the glass wall running along the entire rear of the house at the magnificent sight it offered.

Growing up only Gabriel and Phillip Junior had the rear suites with the glass wall. They were older and got first choice. Sometimes Sean would sleep on one of three sofas in the den, turning the costly furniture into his impromptu bed so that he could look at the view in the moments just before he fell asleep. He had always been fascinated by its beauty. When he eventually moved out one day, he would miss the focal point most of all.

With one last look, Sean continued across the dimly lit den and descended the stately stairs until he reached the first floor into the living room. Even with just lighting offered by the sconces on the walls, there was no denying the beauty of the modern decor of light gray and steel blue found throughout the entire home. It blended with the features common to its Victorian-era architecture with modern upgrades that were undoubtedly beautiful, luxurious and filled with amenities like its own movie theater with a deluxe snack bar, wine cellar, library, safe room with a secret entry and fully stocked pantries on each level.

And of course, the chef's kitchen.

Sean made his way past the door to the half bath on his right and down the brief hall to the kitchen with its pale walls and dark cabinetry, complete with an island near the high-end range and refrigerator. The spacious area opened up to the dining room straight ahead and a den to its left, but it was clear which of them was the showcase. Instantly, he felt some of his concerns ease. Cooking was always his safe place and his peace.

Sean checked the pantry and the fridge before deciding to try something he was considering putting in his new cookbook focused on sandwiches from around the world, including sections on bread making and homemade condiments. His team at Cress, INC. had been suggesting various recipes for him to put his own spin on, and he was curious to see just what he could do with their latest recommendation.

He turned on some jazz music very low and got lost in the art of cooking. He lost track of time as he created every aspect of the sandwich from scratch, including the demi baguettes. No detail or extra step was considered unnecessary. Every element was lightly seasoned before being brought together. For the fried meat, instead of standard sausage or beef, Sean used a Cress, INC. cast-iron pan to sear a fine cut of Wagyu beef with a marbling score of twelve that meant the meat would be spectacularly tender by default. For the *frites*, or fries, he chose sweet potatoes instead of white. All of the vegetables were chopped from skills learned during the early days of all of the brothers working in their parents' various kitchens over the years before leaving to attend culinary school. For the traditional sauces he chose to make a robust garlic sauce and then a gentle béarnaise sauce of butter, egg yolks, vinegar, shallots, peppercorns and tarragon.

"Oh. It's you, Mr. Cress."

Sean looked up from thinly slicing red cabbage to find the family's housekeeper, Felice, standing at the top of the polished wood stairs leading down to the finished basement. The middle-aged woman was still in her robe and obviously freshly awakened from her sleep. He gave her a smile begging for forgiveness. "Sorry, Felice. Felt like cooking," he explained before tossing a hand towel over his shoulder and swiftly turning to remove the baguettes he sliced and then pan grilled in garlic butter.

"Of course," she said, covering a yawn with the

back of her hand. "I'll stay up and clean up once you're done."

Sean frowned. "No, you won't. I'll clean up, but you will try this for me," he said, taking a baguette and filling it with thin slices of the steak that he let rest so that its juices drawn to the center of the meat during cooking would be redistributed and increase its flavor profile. He topped it with the tossed smoked gouda, arugula, red onion, thin slices of carrots and red cabbage, a drizzle of the garlic sauce and then the sweet potato *frites*, which he topped generously with the béarnaise.

"That does look good, Mr. Cress," Felice said, having watched him intently.

He placed the sandwich on a plate and then the plate onto a tray with a bottle of flavored seltzer from the fridge before handing it to the woman with a nod of thanks. "Let me know what you think. In the morning," he stressed before turning to assemble two more of the sandwiches.

"Good night, Mr. Cress," she said before turning to make her way back up the stairs.

He was alone again. The cooking was complete and his focus instantly shifted back to Montgomery and the baby. Needing a new diversion, he focused on washing the pans he used and then cleaning the stove and countertops.

I'm pregnant, Montgomery had revealed.

He paused in wiping down the large island.

"Sean?"

He smiled as he looked up at his youngest brother, Lucas, walking into the kitchen in his own monogrammed robe—gifts from their mother. Of all his brothers, he and Lucas were the closest even though they were six years apart.

With the addition of Lincoln as the new eldest brother, it was Phillip Junior, himself, Gabriel, Coleman and then Lucas. As kids he had been as close to Phillip Junior as Gabriel and Coleman were—not just brothers but best friends. As the baby, and the last child his mother knew she would bear, Lucas had become "The Favorite," undeniably. Coleman was "The Rebel." Gabriel reigned as "The Good One" and Sean was "The Star." Lincoln was "The New One" and Phillip Junior, once "The Eldest," was now—in his mind anyway—"The Heir to the Throne."

And he'd felt that way long before Lincoln's addition to their lives, making Phillip Junior more arrogant and unbearable as the brothers got older—especially with their father stepping down from the business one day. It was then Sean began to spend more time with their little brother as adults. Their shared sense of humor made them friends. With Lucas, he could and would discuss anything.

"Couldn't sleep?" Sean asked as his brother came over to look down at the sandwiches.

Lucas gave him a sheepish smile as his stomach grumbled loudly. "I came down for a snack," he said as he rubbed his flat belly.

"Perfect timing," Sean said, motioning with his chin toward the two sandwiches on the now-spotless island.

Lucas gave it a long look and wiped his mouth with his hand as if it watered, but he shook his head. "If I eat like this at two in the morning, I will gain back all the weight I lost," he said. "And that's not happening."

Sean understood.

As a part of their mother's devotion to her youngest son, Nicolette had given him plenty of affection and even more delectable treats as he stuck to her side like a shadow. Until a few years ago, Lucas had carried sixty extra pounds on his tall frame. And being a skilled pastry chef who loved his own treats, he found it had been no easy feat to lose the weight.

"It's not always what you eat but the portion size and the frequency," Sean reminded him, taking a knife to cut one of the eight-inch sandwiches in half. "Plus, I want your take on it."

"For the cookbook?" Lucas asked, giving it another long look before finally shifting his eyes up to his older brother.

"Possibly," Sean said, turning to pull two bottles of beer from the fridge to open both before setting them on the island.

Lucas frowned as he eyed the frosty bottles. "What's wrong?" he asked.

He knows me too well.

Sean attended parties and led a fast-paced lifestyle, but he was typically a light drinker. Thus, reaching for a beer was a tell he was unable to bluff. Besides, he didn't want to. He needed to unload. He walked over to close the door leading to the cellar. "I may have a baby on the way," he admitted.

Lucas stared at him before his eyes widened as if he needed a moment to process the news. He reached for one of the bottles of beer to take a long drink of it. "Details," he ordered before reaching for the sandwich to take a healthy bite.

"What you have, Chef, is a Belgium sandwich—a *mitraillette* or submachine gun," Sean said.

"Seriously, Sean," Lucas drawled.

He smiled at his brother. "I know," he said with a half smile.

"It's delicious, by the way," Lucas added. "But tell me, who's the mother?"

"Montgomery," Sean admitted, as her words seemed to haunt him.

I'm pregnant.

Lucas's eyes widened in surprise. "Beautiful woman," he said.

"Very," Sean agreed, thinking of her.

"But do you want her to be the mother of your child?" Lucas asked as he turned and crossed the kitchen to the cabinets lining the wall to open a drawer and remove linen napkins.

"I'm not ready for *any* woman to have my child," Sean said with a heavy breath before pushing his half of the sandwich away.

Over the past week his appetite had faded.

Lucas picked up the last piece of his sandwich and dragged it through the sauces that had dripped onto the plate. "But if Montgomery *is* pregnant?" he asked before easing the food into his open mouth.

"Then nothing will ever be the same for either one of us," Sean admitted.

"True," Lucas agreed, dropping the napkin atop the plate. "Anyone else know?"

Sean shook his head. "Not yet. She's waiting to

hear back from her doctor to confirm the at-home pregnancy test," he explained.

Lucas took a sip of his beer. "Soon?" he asked.

"The sooner, the better," Sean said.

"Whatever you need from me, I'm here," Lucas promised him. "Including a lifetime subscription to condoms."

"Noted."

"At least the drama concerning the sex tape is dying down," Lucas offered.

A small reprieve.

Sean shrugged one shoulder. "And provides evidence that I do in fact wear condoms," he said, feeling slightly devilish.

Lucas picked up the napkin to throw it onto his brother's face. "That was way more of you than *anyone* needed to see," he said with a wince.

Sean chuckled.

The elevator in the corner of the kitchen slid to a stop. The brothers both looked toward it to see their mother opening the wrought iron gate.

Great.

It was very possible that Nicolette Lavoie-Cress, chef extraordinaire, philanthropist, devoted wife and their mother, might have heard at least a part of their conversation.

God forbid.

She was as beautiful as she was overly protective of her sons—even Lincoln, as her stepson, had been accepted and was doted upon as well. She looked beautiful and elegant in an azure silk robe with lace trim that could almost be an evening gown. Her silver hair only had hints of her once-blond strands, and her favorite color was blue to match her eyes. She was aging well and looked younger than her years. And her love for their tall and broad father born in a small town in England with skin the color of chocolate was unwavering.

"Impossible de dormir?" Lucas asked her in her native French, wanting to know if she was unable to sleep.

"I called the hospital to check on your father and decided I needed something more than the snacks in the pantry for *le casse-croûte*," Nicolette said, her French accent still prominent.

"Try this for a snack," Sean said, offering her the remaining sandwich with a wave of his hand.

Nicolette arched a silver eyebrow as she came to stand beside Lucas, his height nearly two feet above her own. She pulled the platinum-rimmed plate closer before opening the sandwich to inspect it. "A *mitraillette*?" she guessed, eyeing each of her sons with a twinkle in her eyes.

Sean chuckled. *"Oui*, Chef," he said.

"This shall do very nicely," she said with a smile before pressing the sandwich flatter with her palm and then lifting it to take a bite.

Their parents were two of the top chefs in the world, and to watch her take a bite of his food took Sean back to the days of culinary school awaiting the opinion of his teacher. When their *maman* released a soft grunt of pleasure and did a little shimmy, Sean knew she approved. She took another bite and he knew she loved it.

For him that made it a definite addition to the cookbook.

Nicolette looked at him as she used the linen napkin to pat the corners of her mouth. "My wild son," she said. "Charming, handsome, funny, talented and a star. But also, since you were a child, a dimpled rascal who loved chasing pretty little girls and giving them kisses. Women have always been your weakness."

"True," Sean agreed, unable to deny that he had enjoyed seeing just how many ladies he could woo with his dimples.

A lot of times they tried to woo him.

He gave his mother that winning smile.

"Charmer," she muttered, reaching up to lightly pat his face.

When her hand lingered, he knew she fought the urge to put a little more weight into her pat because of the sex tape scandal.

"Tu es le seul à ne pas t'installer. Allez-vous?" she asked him softly with her eyes filled with regret.

"You are the only one who will not settle down. Will you?" she had asked in French.

He smiled but it was fake because it hid the guilt and concern he had because settling down or having a child was indeed not what he wanted.

Bzzzzzzzzz.

He and Lucas shared a look as Nicolette reached into the pocket of her robe to remove her cell phone. "It's Gabe!" she gasped, looking up with excited eyes. "The baby is coming. I'm heading to the hospital."

Collette, Phillip Junior and Raquel's daughter who was named after Nicolette, was the heart of the family, but also the lone grandchild. She would enjoy another kid to play with.

Like mine.

"Another Cress grand. What a blessing," Nicolette said, picking up the *mitraillette* before quickly moving to the elevator, presumably to get dressed.

"A blessing indeed, *Maman*," Lucas said with a long look at Sean that was heavy with meaning.

If Montgomery is pregnant with my child, will she be as happy for me as she is for Gabe?

Considering the circumstances, Sean found that hard to believe.

The next morning, dressed in red flannel pajama bottoms, a pink fitted thermal top and woven socks adorned with snowflakes, Montgomery sat on the bottom step of the stairwell of the two-story colonial home she inherited from her grandparents upon their deaths nearly five years ago. She looked around at the brightly lit home. She wished she had the time to strip the paint from the wood to expose the beams and trim. To her, the massive brightly colored area rug that anchored the modern fuchsia sofa would work better with wood than the stark white walls.

Although the home was a classic beauty, it was forever in need of repairs and modernization with closed-concept smaller rooms. Just two months ago Montgomery paid out five figures to replace the roof. A year ago the clay sewer pipes that were commonplace during the era of the home's creation were cracked by tree roots and had to be replaced and their layout shifted to meet current city standards. The memory of its cost still made her flinch. Each and every time.

Her to-do list lengthened. Time, effort and money were constantly being poured into the home.

"You're all set, Go-Go."

Montgomery looked back over her shoulder at her father closing the door to the basement before walking over to her as he cleaned his hands on an old piece of torn cloth. She smiled at his nickname for her. As a baby she was always so active. Constantly moving and on the go.

Go-Go.

"I already feel the heat coming back on, Daddy. Thank you," she said, rising to press a kiss to his bearded cheek.

Reverend Alton "Rev" Morgan was a tall and thin man who was as strict with what he ate as he was with the actions he took in the world. Excess was not his forte.

He shifted his wire-framed glasses on his broad nose but looked over the rim at her. "It's the boiler. You're going to need a new one soon," he said with a booming voice that seemed to shake the rafters of his church every Sunday.

Another bill.

She could almost hear it ring up.

Cha-ching.

She hated it but she would pay it. The five-bedroom, four-thousand-square-foot structure was her home and she loved living in Passion Grove, New Jersey. The town offered a slower-paced, small-town feel but was close enough to midtown Manhattan to allow a daily commute into the city to work. Although her home was on the lower end of some of the estates in the town worth millions, she enjoyed the luxury lifestyle set by her wealthier neighbors. The townspeople enjoyed the holidays with events meant to draw them together. For her, after a long day in the busy and congested streets of Manhattan, coming home to Passion Grove, with its heart-shaped lake and streets named after flowers, was ideal.

Now, if I can only get the house to be perfect as well.

"Waking up without heat was not fun. Thanks for coming to my rescue," she said, wrapping her arms around one of his as she walked with him to the front door.

"Always," he said. "Why did you wait until morning?"

"I was fine, Daddy," she said. "I didn't want to wake you in the middle of the night."

Still, he frowned with disapproval.

Please not a speech.

"Hungry?" Montgomery asked, although she knew the answer. It was a trick to divert him.

He never ate before ten o'clock and it was just a little after eight.

"No. Too early for me," Reverend Morgan said, pausing to look around at the house. "You took down that picture of your grandparents over the fireplace."

"Yes. It's in my office. I'd like to think they were looking over me always and were proud of me," she said.

The real me. Not the act I put on for you.

He grunted.

Montgomery loved her father, but she resented that he wouldn't like the person who she truly was and only the one she pretended to be for him. She often wondered if it would have been any different had her mother not passed away when she was just a toddler. Would she have been free from his rules and high expectations? Allowed to get dirty as a child? Able to hang out with friends? To have fun?

"I better get going," he said.

Montgomery reached around him to pick up an insulated tumbler on the half table in the foyer. "How about coffee to take with you on the ride back to Brooklyn?" she asked. "Dark. Four sweeteners. Just the way you like it."

Her father took the coffee and gave her a smile before nodding his head in approval. "That's my girl," he said. "What are you getting into today?"

Waiting for a call from my doctor.

Yesterday she barely made it to a late appointment and while waiting for it to begin the doctor had been called away to an emergency at the hospital with a patient in labor. Montgomery was given an ultrasound, had had blood work and was asked the routine questions before being assured she would hear from the doctor the next day.

Overnight she was nagged with concerns that if she wasn't pregnant there could be other health issues causing the false negative result.

Like a tumor.

"I have a light workday so I'm going by the hospital to check on my friend who had her baby late last night," she said, able to feel excited for Monica who had become a good friend.

It was seeing Sean again that she dreaded. The awkwardness between them was evident. Just a couple of days ago, as she worked alongside him at a photo shoot for his book cover, it felt strained. Like neither knew what to say as they awaited her appointment with her OB/GYN.

"Which friend? Do I know her *and* her husband?" he asked, his brows creased.

You're worrying about my friend and I might be having a baby of my own.

Montgomery fought the urge to press a hand to her flat belly. "No, you don't know the couple," she explained, seeing him instantly relax at the assurance that Monica was not a single mother. "She's one of my clients."

To see how quickly he imposed his opinion on a stranger just reminded her that his judgment of her would only be tenfold. She hated that she was a grown, successful businesswoman who was self-sufficient, and her father still made her feel like a teenager afraid of being called to the carpet for letting him down. But he did. For her father she had always ensured he thought of her as nothing less than perfect.

Admitting to him that she was unwed and pregnant by a man like Sean Cress—about whom nothing said fatherhood—was daunting for her.

"What's wrong, Go-Go?" her father asked as his eyes searched her face. "You'll have your turn to be a wife and a mother. Be patient. It's all on God's time."

Montgomery stiffened and looked up at her father as she forced a smile to cover what felt to be an alarmed expression on her face. "Be safe, Daddy," she said, reaching past him to open the front door.

She shivered as the cold winds instantly wrapped about them.

"You missed church last week, Montgomery," he said, his voice censorious. "That was disappointing. I hope to see you there Sunday."

"Do you want to know why I missed church?" she asked, feeling that confidence she used every day in her successful career rise up in her.

"Were you sick and shut in?" he asked.

No.

Instead, she said nothing.

"Then nothing else matters," he said with a stern look.

It was pure hilarity that she gave her employees and those she encountered during work the same stare to get prime results. With anyone *but* her father.

Growing up it felt like if she said she was going right, he would demand she go left. And in time, to not feel strangled by his rules, she had learned to be misleading. It was then she found her freedom. While studying at New York University for her double major in communications and marketing with a minor in Spanish, Montgomery had truly found her wings living on campus and being out from under the ever-watching eye of Reverend Morgan.

"Yeah, you're right," she said, again relenting to him.

"Be safe. Love you," he said before turning to leave.

"Love you, too, Daddy," she said with a rub to his

back as she gently guided her father out of the house. She looked out the front window of the living room at him climbing behind the wheel of his Cadillac crossover before he pulled away.

Montgomery turned and made her way up the stairs for a hot bath. Halfway up, she took a misstep and stumbled forward on the steps. She was surprised by her cry of dismay as she quickly reached out to grip the step and prevent herself from falling onto her belly. She twisted her body to sit on the step with her heart pounding as she covered her face with her hands. Tears rose at the thought of accidentally falling down the stairs and causing a miscarriage.

In that moment the idea of that happening flooded her with fear and misery.

She pressed one hand to her belly and ran the other through the length of her hair.

She didn't know if she was being foolish to feel so protective of a baby she wasn't even sure existed. Still, it was possible and that was enough for her to be shaken to her core. A miscarriage was not the answer. That would fill her with more regret than her fear of being judged by her father and left to do it alone by Sean.

Montgomery released a long breath and rose to turn and make her way up the stairs. In her bathroom she enjoyed a long warm bath. In the full-length mirror, wearing nothing but her robe opened at the sides, she pictured herself swollen with child. With a shake of the head at herself, she closed her eyes at her own mixed feelings. When she opened them again, there was a vision of Sean standing in the mirror behind her with his hands splayed on her rounded belly.

Montgomery blinked to rid herself of the image.

Silly girl.

Sean didn't want children, and Montgomery didn't want Sean. He was only good for cooking and sex—*really* good.

Okay. Exquisite. The man was magnificent in bed and the kitchen.

But not at fatherhood and commitment.

The loud ringing of her cell phone startled Montgomery. She rushed into her bedroom to pick it up from its charging pad on the nightstand. "Dr. Fletch," she said, reading the name of the incoming caller.

"Here we go," she said, sinking down onto the side of the bed as she answered the call and pressed the phone to her ear.

Come what may, I will make the best of it. Just like always.

Three

Sean stood still under the production tent as the stylist arranged the collar of the navy wool peacoat up around his face. The entire team of his show stood outside one of the dozen CRESS restaurants across the world. For each of the dozen shows in the new season, Sean cooked dinner for a celebrity who was connected in some way to each of the cities in which the eateries were located. They were filming the final episode at CRESS XI on the port of Honfleur in Normandy, France.

Sean looked down at the cute brunette with green eyes as she stepped back to eye the matching shirt and dark denims he wore. With a nod, she approved of her work. "Feel good?" she asked, pulling a lint roller from the black apron she wore to swipe at the coat.

"Feel great," he said.

She gave him a lingering look, but Sean looked away to keep it professional. He didn't date in the work pool. Even as a charmer who loved the company of beautiful women, Sean was not interested in crossing lines at work. He loved his career too much to risk it.

But…had he met her elsewhere he would have gladly accepted the subtle flirtation.

Because of the light rain, the stylist opened an umbrella and handed it to him.

"Ready to shoot, Sean," an assistant said.

The director, Julien Dubois, came up to him. "I actually think the overcast and rain against the backdrop of the harbor will make for a brilliant shoot. *Magnifique!* Yes?" he asked, his French accent heavy. *"Cadre trés intimiste."*

Very intimate setting.

Sean nodded in agreement.

"Let's go," the director said, clasping his hands before turning and walking away.

Sean bit back a smile. Working with the man for the past few days had been a joy. He was in his sixties but had the spirit of a twenty-something lover of life.

Following the instructions of the director, Sean walked up the brief length of the harbor under his umbrella as the camera crew used a track to dolly out away from him. "Welcome to an all-new episode of *Tablemates*, my opportunity to cook a delicious meal of their selection for some of the biggest celebrities across the world," Sean said, walking over to the SUV sitting outside the brightly lit restaurant that seemed to glow against the darkness caused by overcast skies.

"Today join me at the beautiful CRESS XI, here at the port of Honfleur in Normandy, France, as I introduce you to my tablemate…Delphine Côté."

Sean stood on his mark, giving a smile and nod to the uniformed driver standing by the rear door holding his own black umbrella to protect him from the light rain. The man opened the door and extended his gloved hand to assist the acclaimed veteran actress from the vehicle. Delphine had been a recluse for the past twenty of her ninety years of life, but accepted the offer to be on the show at Sean's personal invite.

"*Bonjour*, Delphine," Sean said, stepping forward to bend and kiss both her cheeks before extending the crook of his arm to her.

"*Bonjour*, Chef," she said with a twinkle in her eyes.

"Today we'll spend the day cooking and then dining on your favorites—Basque seafood stew, roast duck and *tourtière landaise* or apple and Armagnac phyllo pie," Sean said as the camera recorded them walking together under his umbrella toward the steps of the restaurant.

"Sounds delicious, Chef," Delphine said.

He held the door for her and she entered as he looked back over his shoulder into the camera. "Join me for another episode of *Tablemates*," he said before lowering the umbrella and dashing inside.

"Cut!" Julien shouted.

Sean smiled down at Delphine. "Thank you for today. It will make the perfect finale," he said in fluent French.

"This should be fun," she said with a pat of her hand atop his before turning to follow a production assistant and her nephew, a tall and thin man who obviously doted on his legendary aunt.

Sean allowed his stylist to take the umbrella from him before removing the overcoat. She placed a custom navy apron that matched his shirt over his head and carefully tied it at the waist. He looked around the restaurant whose creation his brother Gabriel had personally overseen. It was stunning with its high ceilings, minimal decor and unique lighting fixtures that all made the views of the harbor the focal point via the tinted glass walls. In every bit of it he saw his brother's love for the project—and perhaps his love for Monica during those early, more tumultuous days of their relationship.

During the shoot, that took the entire day, he enjoyed himself but his thoughts were on hopping on to the Cress family jet and heading back to New York.

Sean picked up his wineglass and raised it in toast to Delphine where they sat across from one another at a table in the front of house. She raised her glass to touch to his. That was an organic moment. "Thank you for being my tablemate this evening. The company far outshined the meal. *Saluer*," he said with warmth.

Salute.

"Saluer," Delphine repeated.

The cameraman pulled back from their table and then panned up to the sight of the rain against the window.

"Cut!" the director yelled.

Delphine gave Sean a wink before relaxing and leaning back against her chair. "It's been a long time since I allowed cameras in my life. For that meal and your company, it was worth it, Sean," she said before rising to her feet with an agility he hoped to have in his later years.

"Merci," he said.

"Oh my, you're grand," Delphine sighed in pleasure.

Sean smiled bashfully and prepared to thank the woman until he looked up and saw she was instead talking to Gabriel's best friend, Lorenzo León Cortez, a tall, stoic man of mixed Native American and Mexican heritage. His smile faded just a little bit as he was used to being the one to receive compliments.

Lorenzo chuckled deeply. *"Merci beaucoup. Vous êtes assez grand vous-même,"* he said in fluent French although Spanish was his native tongue, thanking her for the praise and bestowing the same upon her as well.

With one last smile up at the man dressed in all black, Delphine followed the production assistant out of the restaurant to her trailer.

Lorenzo and Gabriel had met in cooking school and became fast friends. In time, the family had come to accept him as a close family friend. There had been strain between him and Coleman when his brother assumed Lorenzo was pursuing Jillian before their secret love affair had been revealed. Thankfully, the misunderstanding was cleared and all was well with the men— for which Gabriel had been more thankful than anyone.

"Good show," Lorenzo said. "What I saw of it."

Sean picked up his goblet again to finish the rest of the wine in one deep gulp as the camera crew's talking and actions rose and echoed around them as they began to wrap the day of shooting. "Thanks, Zo," he said. "I almost forgot you were catching me back to the States."

Lorenzo was the head chef of CRESS V on the Champs Élysées in Paris. As the newly appointed godfather of Gabriel and Monica's baby, he was headed to New York to meet his goddaughter.

"I'm all set. Give me a sec," Sean said, rising from his seat.

Lorenzo walked over to the door of the restaurant out of the fast-moving fray.

As Sean thanked the crew for the hard work and nodded in thanks at their applause, he noticed several eyes on his adopted brother before he made his way across the restaurant. He paused to speak to the director, the producers who were on set, and to give the stylist authorization to purchase the entire outfit he wore before he finally pulled on the overcoat and made his way to the door.

"Let's roll," Sean said to Lorenzo.

Both men left the restaurant and dashed out to the chauffeured SUV. There was a couple dozen people waiting in the rain by the vehicle. With a chuckle, Lorenzo got into the rear of the vehicle while Sean took the time to pose for pictures and sign autographs before climbing into the vehicle as well.

"You know, I really need to convince you to do a show for the streaming service once I get it set up," Sean said. "The ladies couldn't take their eyes off you."

"Oh no. I'll stick to cooking. You can have the fame, superstar," Lorenzo assured him with a deep voice.

"It has its benefits," Sean told him with a mischievous wink.

Lorenzo gave him a steady look. "Yes, I heard," he said, obviously referring to the sex tape.

Sean laughed, but then abruptly stopped. "Please don't bring that up around my parents?" he asked with the utmost seriousness.

It was Lorenzo's turn to find humor. "Trust me, Gabe gave me the heads-up."

Good.

"La Havre Octeville, si vous plait." Sean requested in French for the driver to take them to the nearby airfield. The family's private plane awaited, fueled and ready to jet to America. *"Merci."*

The driver nodded and pulled away, careful of the people still standing near the vehicle to get a sight of the famous and beloved Cress family brother.

Sean gave them all a wave through the glass before reaching for the small locked carry-on already on the seat awaiting him as instructed. In it were the clothes he wore that morning, his briefcase, iPad and phone. He had so many missed calls, texts and emails.

None from Montgomery.

Perhaps I should call her?

He looked out the window at the sight of the rustic medieval town.

Or maybe no news is good news?

He remembered the sight of her beautiful face by the light of his phone in the dark interior of the elevator. The way her feline-like eyes searched his just before he saw her desire for him in the depths of hers. Just before they shared one hell of a kiss.

The memory of it and the sparks it set off made his gut clench.

Montgomery had the type of beguiling beauty that

was hard for him to deny. There was something about her that made her stand out in a crowd to him. His eyes would always land on her when they were at an event together. But her demeanor had always been so cool and professional. So unapproachable and formidable.

Until the elevator.

But that version of the woman was gone. He had discovered a new facet to her. The fire. The release. The passion.

His view of her was forever changed.

Sean tapped his phone against his knee before he began to return calls and emails as Lorenzo withdrew a hardcover book and began reading in silence. Soon work became Sean's focus. So much that he was surprised when the vehicle slid to a smooth stop on the paved tarmac of the airfield. He flew in that morning for filming and was headed right back out. As the driver held the door for him, Sean gave him a thankful nod. The men continued across the airfield and up the steps of the sleek black Desault Falcon capable of flying up to twelve people in luxurious comfort.

The uniformed pilot and flight attendant awaited them just outside the cockpit.

"Welcome aboard, Mr. Cress and Señor Cortez," the flight attendant said, accepting their carry-ons. "The sleeping quarters have been prepared for you as requested."

"Thank you," Sean said, striding down the long length of the plane to pass the two leather sofas facing each other, a small conference table and entertainment area to reach the fully made queen-size bed. "You good, Zo? I'm tired as hell."

Lorenzo held up his book before sitting on one of the sofas. "This has my attention," he assured him.

Sean barely took the time to remove his shoes and coat before lying down on his side. In the moments before he fell asleep—without work to distract him— he thought of Montgomery. Again. So many things. Her cries of passion. The feel of her body. The beauty of her eyes. Her possibly being pregnant by him while not ready for fatherhood. At all.

Sean released a heavy breath and welcomed the escape of sleep.

"Mr. Cress. Mr. Cress."

He opened his eyes and looked out the window at the airport. Bright lights broke up the darkness of night. Paris was six hours ahead, so it was early evening in New York.

"We've arrived."

Sean looked back over his shoulder at the flight attendant standing beside the bed. "Thank you," he said, hearing the sleep that thickened his voice.

The smile and the look in the woman's eyes were soft and welcoming.

Sean eyed her for a bit and gave her a grin of his own that he knew was a bit wolfish. She really was appealing, and everything hinted at a night of sexual wonder.

She's no Montgomery.

Sean's eyes widened a bit in shock at that thought.

Since when was Montgomery the epitome of what was desirable to him?

That night.

The attendant's eyes filled with concern. "Is everything okay?" she asked.

Sean sat up and swung his long legs over the side of the bed. "Sorry," he mumbled when she stumbled back to avoid colliding with him.

He slid on his shoes before rising with his coat in hand. He was thankful when she gave him an odd look before quickly making her way to the front of the plane. He pulled on his coat and followed suit. Lorenzo had already disembarked.

"Welcome home, Mr. Cress," the pilot said.

"Feels good to be home," Sean said, accepting his carry-on from the attendant and making his way down the stairs to his awaiting all-black SUV.

The winter winds were crisp and brutal, seeming to reach his bones as he ducked his head and quickly strode across the apron as his driver, Colin, took his case and held the rear door for him. Sean was thankful for the heat of the vehicle as he visibly shivered.

Colin placed their luggage in the rear before moving quickly to reclaim the driver's seat and drive them away. "It's supposed to hit the low twenties tonight. Missing Paris, gentlemen?" Colin asked with a chuckle.

"Yes," Lorenzo exclaimed, rubbing his bare hands together.

"Nope," Sean said without hesitation.

He *loved* New York.

The bright lights and fast pace. Something was always happening in the city. People were always awake. Life was constantly moving. There was an energy—a vibe—that was unmatched.

There was always something—or someone—to do.

"Where to, Mr. Cress?" Colin asked.

"Lenox Hill Hospital."

"Right away," the driver assured him.

Lorenzo dug back into his book.

Sean removed his tablet and began swiping through the list of streaming services and live television stations that might be viable for purchase to become CressTV. He studied each one from their current logo to programming and cost. His team at Cress, INC. had been meticulous in their research and Sean was interested in the streaming service with the easiest transition—even absorbing their employees to not disrupt people's livelihood.

He felt confident that Cress TV would lead to him being appointed CEO of Cress, INC. and afforded the ability to propel the company forward without having to garner the approval of his father who, at times, was against any efforts made to do things differently.

The SUV slowed to a stop outside the hospital.

Sean moved quickly to place his tablet back inside his briefcase. "I'll be a couple of hours. Car is yours. Careful of my case back here," Sean said before climbing out of the rear of the SUV before the driver could leave his seat.

Lorenzo did the same.

Quickly, they made their way inside. Neither man noticed the appreciative looks they drew from the women they passed. After retrieving a visitor's pass, Sean and Lorenzo made their way to Monica's private maternity suite. Sean paused in the doorway at finding Montgomery sitting beside the bed holding his niece. She looked up and their eyes met. And held.

His heart hammered at the very sight of her. And seeing her holding a baby shook him.

"Emme, it's your uncle Sean and godfather Zo!" Monica softly exclaimed from the bed as she leaned over to ease back the baby's blanket. "I wasn't expecting you, Sean. I thought you'd be tired from your trip."

And I wasn't expecting Montgomery.

Sean shifted his eyes from Montgomery with reluctance. "I just got back and came straight here," he said. "I slept on the plane."

"How'd the shoot go?" Gabriel asked from behind him.

Sean turned to find his younger brother sitting at a table in the corner with blueprints laid out before him. "Without a hitch," he assured him, taking another glance back at Montgomery that he couldn't resist as he walked over to look down at the plans. "The new restaurant?"

Gabriel nodded and turned the plans on the table to face his brother. "Cress XIII. Dubai," he said. "Coming 2024."

"Wow," Sean said at the scope and size of the project.

"Go big or stay home," Gabriel said.

Sean nodded. "Damn right," he agreed, turning each page of the blueprint.

"It has me considering leaving Paris to head chef there," Lorenzo said with a broad smile of admiration at the project.

"Oh no, Zo," Monica said from behind them.

The three men looked at her.

"Emme needs all her family and that includes her

godfather. Paris is far enough, *Gabe*," she said, giving her husband a meaningful look to stop his friend's contemplation of moving to Dubai.

"He's a grown man, babe" was all Gabriel said.

Sean looked at Montgomery as she looked down at the baby.

Something tugged at him. Something deep.

Montgomery looked up and locked her eyes on him. "Sean, can I talk to you really quick?" she asked.

His eyes searched hers, looking for some clue.

Are we having our own baby?

"Yeah," he said, clearing his throat.

Lorenzo removed his coat and washed his hands before walking over for Montgomery to ease the bundle of joy into his arms. He claimed the seat she vacated to follow Sean out of the suite. He noticed she was carrying her briefcase and assumed it was work related. As she walked down to the end of the hall, his eyes dipped to take in the motion of her hips in the yellow slacks she wore with a matching V-neck sweater with blouson sleeves.

Montgomery turned to face him when she reached the lone window.

There was a look in her eyes. It was serious. More than usual.

And he knew before she even said the words.

More, Sean. Give me more, he remembered.

It seemed he had given her far more than either bargained for.

"I am pregnant, Sean," she said.

The news didn't weaken him as he thought it would. Perhaps because there had been time to get used to the idea. He nodded as she studied him even as his heart thundered. He looked down at her belly.

"It's yours," she assured him.

He jerked his eyes up to her face.

"And I'm having it," she continued.

Sean nodded again. Letting her guide the conversation because ultimately it was her body. Their life. But *her* body. That meant something.

"And I have a plan."

"A plan?" he asked, not hiding his confusion as he looked down at her, thinking the bright color she wore brought out the beauty of her bronzed skin and bright eyes.

Montgomery wore her hair up in a top knot, but she reached to twist a twirl at her nape around her finger.

She's nervous. Unsure.

She paced a little in front of him and when she stopped to face him again, gone was the hint of insecurity. She was Ms. Cool, Calm and Collected again. But Sean believed it a facade just like the steadiness he was showing her, even as he felt his own uncertainty.

"Okay, the plan," she said, her voice stern and professional as she reached inside her briefcase and withdrew legal documents.

Sean frowned as he took them.

"I propose a marriage of convenience," she said.

"What?" he exclaimed in total shock.

They both looked around them to ensure they were alone and unheard.

"Just hear me out," Montgomery said.

That took him back to the time she used that same phrase when she convinced him that a press junket was the correct course of action to defeat the scandal of the sex tape. She was in full crisis-control mode.

Ever the publicist.

"Marriage will provide security and legitimacy for our child," she began.

Our child.

"It will help me with the image of propriety on a business and personal level," Montgomery continued. "And help demolish the scandalous playboy image for you as you fight to head Cress, INC."

Sean looked down at the paperwork.

"I've laid out a full plan of marriage and eventual divorce after a year, a prenuptial agreement, a non-disclosure agreement and a promise that the marriage only takes place after a DNA test confirms paternity," she explained, her words crisp and concise. "I'm sure you're the father, but I understand you may need proof. I say let's do a quickie wedding in the next month—"

"Wait!" he snapped and then regretted his sharpness. "Please. Just give me a damn moment."

Montgomery licked her lips as she crossed her arms over her chest. "Sean—"

"Please," he asserted, the edge of the papers now creased in his fist. "Just give me a moment."

She nodded and took a step back from him.

Our child.

"Shit," he swore, turning and striding away.

He paused and turned to eye her. "When did you find out?" he asked.

Her eyes shifted away from his. "This morning," she admitted. With softness.

"You've had all day to wrap your brain around this plan and even draw up paperwork, so forgive me if I need some time, Montgomery," he said.

She nodded in understanding.

Sean looked down at the papers with a shake of his head.

A damn business proposal.

"How's the baby?" he asked, surprising himself.

He looked up and her eyes showed her surprise as well. "So far, so good," she said.

Sean smiled a bit. "Good," he said.

"Yes," she agreed.

"I'll be in touch. Soon," he said before turning and striding away as he rolled the paperwork up in his hands and slid it in the inside pocket of his coat.

He didn't go back to Monica's suite. Instead, he found the elevators to go up to the cardiology ward. When he finally entered his father's room, he paused in the doorway at the sound of his mother singing softly in French about loving him forever.

The sounds of sweet kisses echoed, and Sean backed out of the room.

"Come in, whoever's shadow is on the floor," Phillip Senior said in a booming voice and heavy British accent that seemed to echo in his barrel chest.

With a chuckle, Sean entered the room, closing the door as he stepped inside.

His tall and broad father lay on the bed in a designer bathrobe over his hospital gown. His mother sat on the edge of the bed beside him. They both gave him a look.

Feeling as if their love bubble was being invaded

was a constant for Sean and his brothers growing up. His parents were forever lost in one another. They loved each other, their children and cooking. Together they had overcome difficulties, somehow strengthened their bond and built an empire from whose very existence their children all benefited.

Really, all any parent could do as they grew and matured was the very best they could.

A lesson to remember as a parent-to-be.

"And how was Delphine?" Phillip Senior asked.

"Amazing. And a surprisingly good cook," Sean said, pulling one of the few chairs that lined the pale gray wall to the other side of the bed before sitting. "Perhaps good enough for a cooking show of her own...on Cress TV."

"And is she still a beauty?" Nicolette asked.

Sean nodded. "Yes. She looks sixty or seventy. *Definitely* not ninety," he said.

"Good job getting her on *Tablemates*, son," Phillip Senior said.

Sean felt he sounded weak and tired. A glance at his mother showed her concern as well. "I can come back tomorrow," he said.

"No," Phillip Senior said emphatically before extending his hand. "Don't go yet, son."

Sean's eyes widened a bit as he clasped his father's hand.

Phillip Senior patted his hand. Affectionately.

Sean fought not to stare at the touch.

The Cress brothers were loved and taught to love, but shows of affection were Nicolette's commonplace. Phillip Senior had raised five sons and treated the job as a man raising future men. Tough. Loving. But not overtly affectionate.

There was a change.

Sean was stunned but tried to cover it well.

Nicolette leaned across the bed to pat the side of his face. "My son. I see your shock," she said. "Your father's condition has changed us both for the better."

Phillip Senior grunted. "Damn near dying has a way of doing that," he added.

"And seeing your love damn near die does the same to those who love him," Nicolette continued.

True.

The entire family had been rocked to discover their strong and formidable father passed out on the floor of the townhouse. Then the open-heart surgery, his recovery afterward and the waiting for the all-clear for his release from the hospital. All of it was daunting.

"To continue to do things the same after such an event is madness," Nicolette said. "For me, too."

"We surrender the fight, son," Phillip Senior said, closing his eyes.

"About the business. About the loves of my sons. About being so focused on where you boys lead your life that we stopped focusing on living our own," Nicolette explained as she leaned in to press a kiss to the cheek of her love.

Even with his eyes closed Phillip Senior smiled like a big cuddly bear.

Sean chuckled.

His father's grip on his hand weakened. Sean gripped his instead, wishing he could flood his father with his strength.

"Time to see the world and not just cook dishes from it, my love," Nicolette said.

Phillip Senior nodded in agreement, but it, too, was weak. *"À la nourriture. À la vie. À l'amour,"* he said in a whisper.

It was his mother's favorite saying in her native French tongue. To food. To life. To love.

It had become Cress, INC.'s brand used in some way in every division of the company.

Sean eyed his father.

"He's fine, superstar," Nicolette said. *"Je promets."* I promise.

Sean released his father's hand as he nodded and rose, replacing the seat back to its place, before leaving as his mother began to softly hum.

"Nicolette, let's FaceTime Monica. I want to see Emme before I go to sleep," Phillip Senior said.

"Yes! She gets more beautiful every day. Two grandchildren, my love. Can you believe it?" Nicolette asked.

"With the lot we have it'll be a dozen or better one day," Phillip Senior said. "Won't that be grand?"

Sean paused in the doorway.

And my baby will make three.

He stepped into the hall and closed the door before making his way to the elevator.

I'm going to be a father.

As the doors to the elevator closed, Sean leaned back against the wall and pulled the papers from inside his coat to unroll.

Montgomery was pregnant.

Deep in his heart, he had already known it was true.

Then nothing will ever be the same for either one of us.

He closed his eyes and tapped the papers against his chin. A baby. Fatherhood. But marriage? The idea of that type of union for any length of time was insanity. He was not looking for love or a drastic change in his lifestyle. No more partying? Or dates with any beautiful woman he chose? Checking in with someone about his whereabouts? Not traveling to exotic locales on a whim? No more freedom?

Ding.

"Wake up, little brother."

Sean opened his eyes to find Gabriel and Lorenzo stepping onto the elevator.

"We're going down to enjoy a quick cigar," Lorenzo said. "Join us."

Sean shook his head as he stepped off the elevator. "I have a date with a beauty named Emme," he said before turning to walk to Monica's suite.

He crossed her private waiting room and knocked on the door to her room.

"Come in," Monica called out.

He entered, finding that Montgomery was gone, his niece in her bassinet and Monica sitting her phone down on the bedside table.

"That was your parents," Monica said with a soft smile. "They told me you were probably on your way down."

Sean nodded, coming to stand beside the bassinet to tilt his head to the side as he looked down at the baby silently suckling on the side of her fist. "Can I hold her?" he asked her.

"Of course," Monica said. "I would never say no to any of the uncles. Her protectors. All of you."

Sean scooped Emme into his hands and held her in his arms with a glance at his sister-in-law. Her eyes were damp, but her smile was real.

"She will have the life I never had growing up in foster care. So much love and family," Monica said, swiping at a tear that raced down her cheek. "She'll never be alone."

"And neither will you. Never again." Sean promised this woman his brother deeply loved who had once been a housekeeper in their home and was now one of the family—fitting in like a perfectly cut puzzle piece. "We're family."

Monica nodded in agreement as she reached to squeeze his wrist. "And that matters so much."

Sean looked down into the face of the little brown bundle of joy. When she opened her eyes and then smiled, revealing a dimple so like his own, love for her swelled inside his chest. Just like the devotion he had for Collie. Family. Blood. A connection never to be broken. Love unbound. He *knew*, even with his doubts and hesitations, that his feelings for his child would run even deeper.

In that moment, as he raised his niece enough to snuggle his chin against her cheek and press a kiss to her forehead, Sean knew what he *had* to do.

Four

One month later

"Mr. Cress."

Both Sean and Montgomery looked up at the flight attendant standing between the leather sofas where they sat opposite each other.

"We are still not cleared for takeoff due to inclement weather," the woman who introduced herself as Lili said. "The pilot suggests continuing to wait it out on board so that as soon as he's given the all-clear we can immediately taxi for takeoff."

"Thank you, Lili," Sean said, setting down the tablet on which he had been reading something.

Montgomery eyed his profile. His square jawline and long lashes. The deep maroon cashmere sweater he wore looked delicious against his shortbread complexion and dark hair.

Lili handed each of them a leather-bound binder with the Cress, INC. logo embossed on the front. "Here is the inflight menu, which as you know is catered by CRESS X in Tribeca," she said. "Please let me know if there's anything I can get for you."

"The future Mrs. Cress loves fresh pineapples," Sean said as he opened the binder.

Montgomery paused in looking at the selections, surprised he knew that.

"In fact, we do have fresh fruit," Lili said, looking at Montgomery. "Would you like me to make a plate for you?"

"Yes. Yes, I would actually," she said, looking down at the menu. She was thoroughly impressed. It far surpassed the fare offered on first class flights. "*And* the Caesar salad, sweet potato soup and lamb shank with grilled vegetables."

Sean bit back a smile. "Hungry?" he asked, looking amused.

"Very," Montgomery said as she handed the flight attendant the menu.

"I'll have the sea bass with mashed potatoes and grilled vegetables and black coffee," he said, handing over his menu as well. "And let's do the full setup at the table."

"Of course," Lili said before walking to enter the galley, leaving them alone.

Sean looked down at his Piaget watch. "Besides being ravenous, how are you feeling?" he asked.

"Cravings are cravings," she said. "And I feel fine."

"So we're in full baby mode," he said, his eyes dipping to her stomach.

Montgomery crossed her legs in the fuchsia virgin wool convertible sweater she wore with matching straight-leg slacks. "We woke up late in the pregnancy game, Sean. There's nothing to do but get on board," she said.

"Right," he agreed.

"We're having a baby," Montgomery said, still trying to wrap *her* brain around that as well.

"And getting married," Sean added.

They shared a look.

The feel of his eyes on her warmed her.

Montgomery looked away. She ran from her desire for him. It had gotten her into enough trouble.

Sean accepted her proposal. They completed the DNA test. Signed the papers. And were flying to Vegas to get married.

My father will be livid, but not as much as me being unmarried and pregnant.

"Two questions."

Montgomery cut her eyes over at Sean at his comment. "Fire away," she said, shifting on the seat.

"Is there a thing with the bright colors you always wear?" he asked.

Montgomery looked down at her outfit and then up at him. "My way to live out loud after growing up feeling unseen and unheard as a preacher's kid," she explained.

"A preacher's kid?" he asked, his beautiful eyes widening in surprise.

She nodded. "My father," she said.

"Is that why you wanted to get married?" Sean asked, his eyes studying her.

"Trust me, it's worth it for my peace," Montgomery said.

"Shouldn't I have asked for his permission to marry you?"

"Don't ask for permission. Plead for forgiveness," she said. "He wouldn't have approved it anyway."

Sean looked offended. "I'm a catch!" he spouted.

Montgomery shifted to the edge of the sofa to lean over and pat his knee. "Of course you are," she said consolingly.

Sean did not look appeased.

Reverend Morgan would have wanted months of courtship and a completed premarital course before giving his stamp of approval and there was no time for that.

"Next question," Montgomery said, hoping to divert his attention.

Sean leaned forward as well, placing an elbow on each of his knees and locking his hands in the space between them. "Once again we're stuck together with nowhere to go," he said.

His stare was so intense.

She fought the urge to lick her lips as her pulse raced.

This was the first time she had seen him since they met to do the DNA test. Nothing had changed. She was still affected by him. Turned on by him. He made her feel more alive in those moments just before he neared her.

Her eyes dropped to his mouth but then she shifted

them away, only for them to fall on the queen-size bed in the sleeping area at the rear of the plane. When she looked back to him, his line of vision had followed hers. "Sex is not a part of the deal," she rushed to say.

Sean nodded as he looked back at her. "It can be," he said, his voice deeper than usual. More serious. "It should be."

Even as she shook her head she shivered. "You're free to live your sex life to the fullest as long as you're discreet," she reminded him as she sat back on the sofa needing space from his energy.

It barely helped.

More. Give me more, Sean, she had begged him.

Montgomery was thankful for the thickness of her sweater as her nipples hardened at the memory.

"Let's not pretend that night wasn't amazing," he continued.

Yes. Yes, it was.

For the first time in her life, Montgomery knew what it meant to be fully pleasured. Standing on wobbly legs in that elevator as she rushed to get dressed had been the most difficult of tasks to complete.

"It's up to us just how much we enjoy the next year, wife," he stressed.

"Not yet," she reminded him.

Sean fell quiet and picked up his tablet to swipe the screen.

Montgomery felt like a hypocrite. She was disappointed he had ceased his flirtation and seduction. She tucked her hair behind her ear and picked up her own laptop on the sofa beside her. She focused on the daily clippings of her clients in the press that her assistant emailed her. But her eyes kept going to him. Watching him. Remembering him.

Wanting him.

A year was a long time to live with a man and deny herself pleasure every day.

A very long time.

Being basically alone on the plane, as the crew kept out of sight, was a preview of their life to come. Working together always came with a team of people and tasks to help distract them. Here there was nowhere to hide or run from the attraction.

Just like the elevator.

And when Sean looked up suddenly and caught her eyes on him, his expression changed and his eyes darkened.

He did not hide his desire for her. It was there. Stirring her.

That all-too-familiar pulse charged the air.

He said nothing, but his eyes said it all.

Let's not pretend that night wasn't amazing.

The feel of his tongue circling her nipples. His hands stroking her back and buttocks. Whispers against her skin. Inches stoking deeply inside her.

Montgomery felt breathless and could not look away from him. The chemistry seemed to have a life all its own. With her eyes still locked on him across the short divide, she traced her bottom lip with her finger. His eyes dipped to watch the action before he moved to sit beside her.

The heat of his body and the scent of his cologne teased her.

"Montgomery," he said, low in his throat.

In just him uttering her name was a request to give in to the passion again.

She focused her eyes on her laptop but truly had no clue what she was pretending to read on the screen. She wanted nothing more than to fling the device away and turn to climb onto his lap. She closed her eyes and envisioned him raising the skirt of her dress up around her waist and his hands massaging her plump bottom as he pressed kisses along her neck.

The bud of her intimacy throbbed to life.

She released a little grunt and shifted away from the heat of him. The temptation. His appeal.

Sean Cress was a well-known playboy who seemed to run through women like tissues. His charm and beauty made him desirable. Having enjoyed his skill as a lover made him irresistible.

"Dinner is served," the flight attendant said.

Montgomery jumped to her feet, thankful for the interruption. "I'm starved," she said with a nervous laugh as she pushed her hair back from her face.

"Damn right you are," Sean muttered.

She looked back at him.

"And so am I but to hell with food," he told her.

What would his mouth feel like on me right now? Kissing those *lips. Stroking my clit.*

Montgomery faced forward and moved over to the table to take a seat. She rushed to pick up the glass of iced water for a deep sip that was cold but useless to douse the flame he stoked.

Sean pushed up the sleeves of his sweater as he took the seat across the table from her.

His eyes stayed locked on her as Lili set their steaming plates in front of them before stepping back.

"Let me know if there is anything else you need," the woman said.

Sean removed his napkin and snapped it open from its fold. "What I want only the future Mrs. Cress has," he said, giving Montgomery another intense look before dropping the linen atop his lap.

Lili bit back a smile and left them alone, closing the door to the galley.

"Sean," Montgomery said, hating that her hand trembled so badly that the water quaked inside the glass. She rushed to set it down.

"Do you want me?" he asked, sitting back in the chair as he stroked his fingers across the glossy top of the lacquered wooden table.

"What?" she asked, completely caught off guard.

"Te deseo. Quiero besarte mientras acaricio dentro de ti toda la noche. No he olvidado la primera vez. No puedo olvidarlo. Lo revivo, deseando que hubiera durado más," he said, his Spanish fluent and smooth.

And devastatingly sexy.

She knew he spoke French but not Spanish.

Montgomery minored in the language and dreamt of time to visit Spanish-speaking countries. So she understood him clearly and was shaken to her core.

I want you. I want to kiss you as I stroke inside you all night. I have not forgotten that night. I relive it, wishing it could have lasted longer.

This man. This man. This man.

"Te quiero en la cama debajo de mí con tus piernas envueltas alrededor de mi cuerpo mientras te

monto. No había sitio para eso en el ascensor. Pero lo hicimos funcionar. ¿Recordar?" he asked, taking a sip of his drink as he watched her over the rim of the glass.

Montgomery's heart pounded. Furiously so.

I want you on the bed beneath me with your legs wrapped around my body as I ride you. There was no room for that on the elevator. But we made it work. Remember?

How could she *ever* forget…

Desire conquered fear.

Their kisses and the touch of his hands undressing her released a fiery desire that was undeniable. The feel of the satin dress sliding down her body was like a second caressing hand. Montgomery shivered in pleasure as she clung to Sean, wishing she could see more of him hidden by the darkness. But her hands revealed all as she felt the hard contours of his body beneath his clothes. His broad shoulders. Wide back. Hard buttocks.

Standing in nothing but her strapless lace bra, matching thong and heels, Montgomery flung her head back and reveled in the feel of his tongue against her pulse. "Yes," *she sighed with a moan of pure pleasure.*

He walked them back until she felt the coldness of the wall against her back and buttocks. The shock of it only intensified their heat. She bit her bottom lip as he lowered his body to press kisses everywhere. That deep dip between the curves of her breasts as her chest rose and fell with each hot breath. A deep suck of her hard nipples through the sheer material covering them. Her belly. Navel. Each hip.

Each move sent a jolt of electricity through her body that arched her back from the wall.

"Sean," she whimpered as he used his fingers to ease her thong down over her buttocks and then her hips.

When they dropped atop her feet, she kicked them free.

"Damn," he swore, pressing his face against the clean-shaven plump mound of her femininity.

Lightly, he bit it.

Montgomery cried out.

"You smell good," he moaned against her flesh in the moments just before he slid one leg over his shoulder and opened her lips to taste her.

Her fingers dug into his shoulders and without a bit of control her hips arched forward.

She wished she could look down and see him taste her—enjoy her. His grunts of pleasure echoed in the darkness that was only slightly broken up by the phone that fell to the floor in the corner.

Over the years Montgomery had thought she experienced pleasure, but no one had ever tasted her in that way before. She cupped the back of his head, almost tenderly, as she looked out into the darkness and worked her hips back and forth as he suckled her. It was beyond anything she had ever felt before. So intense. So provocative.

What little restraint she had faded, particularly under the cover of darkness. She gave in. Fully.

Montgomery softly licked her lips. "Make me cum, Sean," she begged.

His body froze at her boldness. And then he went to work fulfilling her request. The rapid flicker of the tip of his tongue sent her right over the edge into bliss. Sweat coated her body and her heart raced as she cried out. Sean was relentless, locking her legs in place as he devoured her, caring nothing for her uncontrollable quivers of her body as she climaxed.

But she was not done.

"Now," she begged, pushing away his face. "Please."

With one last kiss, Sean rose in the darkness. She heard the rustle of his clothing as he undressed. When he reached out for her she met his touch and jerked him closer. He pressed kisses along her shoulder and up her neck to eventually reach her mouth. Their tongues danced against each other before she sucked his into her mouth with a deep moan.

Smoothly, he raised her leg up onto the crook of his arm.

Her hands explored his nudity. Reveled in it. He was so hard and fit.

The tip of his throbbing hardness stroked against her clit as she sought and found the base of his neck to suckle.

His moan of pleasure thrilled her.

The feel of him sliding his hard inches inside her fulfilled her in a way beyond the thickness of him.

With a smile she moved her head to deeply bite one of his shoulders as she raised the leg he held to now rest on his shoulder.

"Wait. Don't move. Don't make me cum. Not yet. Please," he begged, his deep voice evidence of his shivers.

She rolled her hips as she traced her fingers across the muscles of his back and gripped the strength of his buttocks.

"Montgomery," he warned in her ear before pressing a kiss to her cheek.

She turned her head toward him. "So be it. Cum then," she whispered against his mouth. *As she worked her core up and down the tip of his inches.*

"It's so tight. So wet and hot. Damn," he said in a low roar.

"More. Give me more, Sean," she begged, needing the rest of her climax she shifted her hips as he stroked inside her.*

And he did.

Slowly. He filled her deeply.

Montgomery lightly tapped her head against the wall, sure she was slipping into madness.

They moved together. In sync. Honed in to each other. Lost in his strokes, the spin of her hips and the fever of their kisses. Sometimes they rocked together slowly as they breathed in the charged air between and around them. But then they would quicken the pace and clung to each other almost desperately and got lost in one another. His hardness. Her softness. Their cries filled the air and with each stroke, Montgomery's buttocks made a slight pounding noise against the wall.

Thump-thump-thump-thump-thump-thump.

The world seemed to spin off its axis as they fought together for their climax.

Sean's rough cries thundered against the walls of the elevator as Montgomery buried her face against his neck and held him tightly during the entire explosive ride that jerked their bodies and riddled them with a pleasure that craved infinity. And they sought the pleasure until both were still, panting and spent.

Montgomery blinked. She released her reverie to find him still watching her.

"Were you remembering?" Sean asked. "I see it in your eyes. The same desire I felt that night I see in your eyes right now. Why fight it?"

Montgomery fought for the control she treasured and ignored his temptation as she focused on her food. "The soup is just what I need on a cold night like this," she said. "How's your meal?"

Sean chuckled. "Lacking in comparison," he said.

Montgomery crossed her legs, hoping the pressure of her thighs would stop the steady throbbing of the bud of her intimacy—that fleshy button ready to be pushed. She refused to even look directly at him—be drawn to him and tempted by her desire.

Their marriage was her idea. Her machination. Foolishly, she had not calculated her lingering desire for him into the equation.

What have I done?

They continued their delicious meal with her keeping their conversation focused on work. She was thankful that inquiring about his newest culinary show seemed to dull his sexual desire as he spoke of the program he completed that was to be aired the following year. And his excitement was infectious. She found herself asking questions and making suggestions to help promote it. She had assumed Sean Cress—the sexy A-list playboy chef—was in love with himself, but it was becoming clear that he loved the opportunity to share his love for cooking more.

Interesting.

"How was your meal?" Lili asked as she used a tray to remove their plates.

"Delicious," Sean said, sparing her a quick glance and thankful smile.

Montgomery could clearly see just why the man was a star. He was charming, smart, confident and exuded a warmth that made you want to be near him. Close to his vibe. Affected by his upbeat mood.

She covered a sudden yawn with her hand. "I think I need a little nap," she said, rising to her feet.

Sean did the same.

Ever the gentleman.

"You feeling okay?" he asked.

She nodded. "Yeah. A little tired," she said, coming around the table to move back to the sleeping area.

"Will you dream of us?" Sean asked.

Montgomery paused in removing her heels.

Inevitably.

She didn't dare look in his direction. Instead, she lay down on her side and pulled one of the plush pillows to her body to hold. With her eyes locked out the window at the movement of uniformed airport employees in the frigid cold rain, she wondered how the heat of Sean's body would feel beside her. Behind her with his strong frame outlining hers and his hand resting on her belly. His inches hard against her buttocks. His breath softly fanning the hairs of her nape.

And in the moments just before she closed her eyes and drifted to sleep she felt a warm cover draped over her body. "Thank you," she said softly, thinking it was their attentive flight attendant.

The scent of a warm masculine cologne proved her to be wrong.

Montgomery awakened with a stretch and a deep sigh as she rolled over onto her back. When she sat up, she found Sean at the conference table furiously typing away on his laptop. He glanced back at her.

"Hello, sleepyhead," he said.

She flung back the cover and swung her feet over the side of the bed. "Where are we?" she asked.

"We should be landing at the North Vegas Airport soon," he said, watching her as she slipped on her heels.

"I didn't think the weather in New York would ever clear up for us to take off," she said, rising to smooth and arrange her clothing that had twisted in her sleep.

"We took off about an hour after you went down for a nap," Sean supplied before closing his laptop.

She walked the length of the plane to pass Sean and reach the sofa where she had left her own work. Taking a seat, she began to pack her tablet and laptop in her monogrammed briefcase.

"Good thing we won't be sharing a bedroom," he said.

She gave him a curious look. "I agree, but what's your reasoning?" she asked.

"You snore."

Montgomery's mouth dropped open. "The lies you tell, Sean Cress!" she exclaimed.

He laughed and shrugged. "There's no way our baby will sleep well with all that rumbling going on," he quipped.

Montgomery snatched a piece of paper from a notepad and balled it up to fastball over at Sean. He ducked and caught it with one hand.

"Poor kid," he joked.

"Are you being serious?" she asked. "Are you really saying I snore?"

Sean rose to saunter over to the sofa. "Are you really saying you don't know?" he asked, slightly incredulous.

"Sean," Montgomery insisted, wanting to know.

He looked down at her. "Just a low purr and not a loud rumble," he said. "Thank God."

"If it would get you in bed with me you would lie right next to my loud rumble and like it," she shot at him.

"Sure would," Sean agreed with a wink.

Montgomery gave him a playful eye roll before focusing on gathering her things in preparation for their landing. She slid on her cream longline wool coat before sinking back down to the sofa. She was just an hour from becoming Mrs. Sean Cress and seven months from becoming a mother. She released a breath. A heavy one.

All of her plans—her perfectly constructed life— were off the rails.

Everything.

"Hey."

She looked up at Sean now standing beside her.

His eyes searched hers before filling with concern. "No need to panic," he assured her, reaching to grip her shoulder in comfort. "We're in this together and we're doing what's best."

Montgomery nodded in agreement and raised her hand to cover Sean's with her own before briefly leaning her head against his forearm.

"We're preparing to land, Mr. Cress," Lili said.

Sean reclaimed his seat and Montgomery instantly missed the warmth of his touch. The nearness of him.

They landed with ease.

"Enjoy your stay in Las Vegas, Mr. and Mrs. Cress," Lili said as they passed her to deboard.

Montgomery stopped for a moment at that before she continued down the stairs where Sean preceded her. He stopped to extend his hand. Again, she paused and looked around at the airport, the sleek black jet, the high-end SUV sitting on the tarmac and the handsome man awaiting to assist her. This was her life for at least the next year.

Mrs. Cress.

Most women would look forward to the wealth, the luxury and the glamour.

Montgomery did not.

She took Sean's hand as she took the final steps down off the plane. They walked together down the black carpet leading to the SUV as their driver opened the rear door for them to slide onto the heated leather seats.

Sean answered a call on his phone but Montgomery was lost in her thoughts. Her fears.

She didn't want to lose herself in the lifestyle of the wealthy and prominent Cress family. Not for herself or her child. Such affluence, without the proper guidance, love and support, could lead to the ruin of a child growing up in it. Her career as a publicist who helped clean up the messes created by spoiled celebrities made it clear what privilege could do to a person.

I won't let it ruin my—our—child.

Things moved quickly. They drove straight to the Clark County Marriage License Bureau to provide their identification for the license application they completed online. Next, they reached the luxurious five-star hotel resort directly on the Vegas strip and were quickly led to their private suite with marbled floors on the fortieth floor. Sean removed his coat as the hotel porter showed Montgomery around the massive suite. She was stunned by its opulent decor, luxury and size. Her eyes widened at the butler's pantry to her left and a full bathroom to her right. Two-bedroom suites were on either end of the wide hall. The center of the suite had 360-degree views with a living room, wet bar and dining area. She turned as she looked up at the towering tray ceiling with glass inlay.

"What size is this?" she asked the porter.

"The apartment is nearly thirty-five hundred square feet," the man replied.

Montgomery released a low whistle.

"Anything else, ma'am?" the porter asked.

She shook her head.

"Enjoy your stay," he said before exiting the suite.

"Thank you," she said, closing the door.

She turned to cross the hall, finding Sean standing

before the apron window, seemingly in deep thought, with his hands in the pockets of the maroon wool slacks he wore.

After agreeing to a Vegas wedding, Sean told her he would take care of the arrangements. Montgomery had never expected this was his idea of a quick trip to Vegas.

"Sean—"

He looked back over his shoulder. "The officiant will be here in an hour," he said.

"At this late hour?" she asked, checking the time on her watch.

"It's Vegas," he said, splaying his hand as he gave her that smile.

Her heart skipped a beat.

"Which room is mine?" she asked, reaching for the handle of her carry-on sitting by the door. "I want to freshen up."

"The one to your left," Sean said. "And check your closet."

Montgomery frowned. "The closet?" she mumbled as she made her way down the long, well-appointed hall to reach the bedroom suite. "What's in it? A chandelier?"

With a quick glance at the sweeping view of the brightly lit strip against the skies that seemed a dark blue, she crossed the spacious suite to seek out the closet, finally finding it in the entry to the en suite. Opening the frosted double doors, she was taken aback by the sight of at least a dozen white and off-white dresses with five pairs of shoes either satin or embellished with crystals.

"No way," she whispered, stepping in to quickly check the sizes of each one.

It was right.

She stooped to pick up one pair of shoes.

Dead on again.

That man. That man. That man.

She hadn't planned on anything special for the ceremony but it seemed Sean had plans of his own. A huge gesture to her probably was nothing more than a whim to a wealthy man like Sean Cress. Still, the dresses *were* beautiful and regardless of the circumstances, it was her wedding.

Maybe the only one I'll have the way things are going.

She kicked off her shoes and undressed as she made her way across the marbled bathroom to draw a bath. Once she loosely pinned up her hair and sank beneath the steaming depths of the water, she eyed the dresses that ranged from simple to sexy to sequined.

An hour later she emerged from her suite wearing a cream strapless linen-silk midi dress scattered with matching floral applique. The hem of the full skirt floated just across her knees and it fit her frame to perfection. Because the dress was so ornate, she went with a simple but beautiful strappy sandal embellished with gold crystals.

She paused at finding a trail of white rose petals down the hall. A bouquet wrapped with cream silk and a crystal adornment rested on the floor. The sound of a violin filled the air. A photographer stepped into the hall to begin silently snapping pictures.

"What?" she asked in surprise, reaching the bouquet and stooping to pick it up.

As she rose and turned, the lights dimmed and candlelight reigned from seemingly every available spot in the large living area. The trail of rose petals continued and led to Sean standing in front of the Vegas view in a tuxedo that seemed tailored to fit. She barely noticed the officiant take his spot as Sean turned and looked at her. His mouth fell open.

"Wow," he mouthed with an admiring shake of his head. "Beautiful."

And that reaction from him caused her to swoon.

She came down the path made of roses to stand before him, feeling a shyness at the way his eyes never strayed from her. Seemed to caress her. Praise her.

"I hope we have a girl and she looks just like you," he said, his voice warm and his eyes deep.

"Sean, you didn't have to do all this. It's too much," she said, before whispering, "It's not a real marriage. It's—"

He reached to lightly pinch her wrist. "Seems real to me," he whispered back. "Besides, don't we want it to look real?"

She shook her head, amazed that she felt weepy. She wanted nothing more than her Mr. Perfect to have surprised her with such a romantic gesture. Someone who loved her and wanted to spend the rest of his life with her.

"Do you like it?" Sean asked.

"I *love* it," she gushed.

"Then just enjoy it," he urged, reaching for her hand. Montgomery looked around at it all, feeling nervous at the grandeur. The opulence. It was all commonplace for Sean. She made a good living as a top publicist—a very good living—but it was nowhere near the lifestyle of the Cress family.

"I guess this might be too much, too."

She looked at him.

Handsome charmer.

And then she looked down at a Tiffany-blue ring box he held with a wedding band and a perfect diamond solitaire ring inside. It was five carats. If not more.

Montgomery stepped forward and leaned in, her mouth to his ear. "I want us to stay at my house in Passion Grove for the next year," she said, needing balance. Wanting to feel more of herself and her life in the picture they were creating. "It's where I'll live with the baby after our divorce so let's set the routine for it now."

Sean looked confused and squinted his sexy eyes. "Okay," he agreed.

"Okay," Montgomery said, taking that step back forward.

As the officiant performed the ceremony, Montgomery could think of nothing else but the feel of Sean's hand covering hers. Its warmth was comforting. Its heat made her tremble in awareness of him.

"By the power vested in me by the state of Nevada, I pronounce you husband and wife," the officiant said with a smile. "You may now kiss your bride."

Before Montgomery could protest, Sean gripped her upper arms and leaned in. His soft kiss landed to her cheek. She forced a smile as her disappointment of not being kissed by her husband stung.

Five

I should have kissed her.

He took a sip of coffee and eyed Montgomery over the edge of the platinum-rimmed cup as they flew back to New York after an uneventful night in Vegas. Her hair was pulled back in a sleep ponytail with light makeup and she wore a cream wide-leg sweatsuit. She looked surprisingly refreshed. They had enjoyed a late dinner—ribeye, seafood soufflé and garlic broccolini followed by a complimentary one tier wedding cake adorned with fresh flowers—and then focused on work as they lounged on separate sofas before going to bed in the wee hours of the morning.

But even as he tried to focus on monthly ratings reports from Cress, INC. and more details on possible streaming services to acquire, he couldn't forget the first sight of Montgomery when he turned and saw her walking toward him in that dress. She had taken his breath away. It felt as if something clutched his heart, and warmth spread over his body.

And that shook him.

As Montgomery Morgan stood before him looking like something out of a dream, pregnant with his child and just proclaimed as his bride, Sean had been shocked at his hope that it all could be real.

And *that* scared him.

As badly as he wanted to feel the touch of her lips against his, Sean resisted because theirs was a one-year marriage of convenience brought on by an accidental pregnancy. The baby would tie them together for a lifetime, but the marriage would not.

In a year I'll be free again.

Still…

I should have kissed her.

He began to think that moment would be his biggest regret. And perhaps for her as well, because for a second, he thought he saw disappointment in the depths of her feline-like eyes.

"Oh no," Montgomery said, looking up from her laptop.

Sean shifted his eyes away so that she wouldn't catch him staring at her. "What's wrong?"

"Your insane popularity," she said before turning the device around for him to see.

"Celebrity chef Sean Cress weds his publicist, Montgomery Morgan," he read before looking down at the photo of them taken when they entered the hotel the morning of his press junket.

"It's *everywhere*," she said, rising to begin pacing.

Sean closed the laptop and set it on the sofa beside him. "It wasn't a secret, Montgomery," he said calmly.

She whirled to eye him with an incredulous expression.

"The purpose of the marriage was for it to be known to protect you professionally and personally. Remember?" he asked.

"But not like this," she said, coming over to pick up her laptop and drop down on the sofa beside him. "The plan was telling our families first."

"The best laid plans of mice and men often go awry," Sean quoted the line of the well-known poem.

"That seems to be my life story lately," she muttered with a twist of her lips showing her annoyance.

He laughed. "No worries, wife," he said with teasing.

"Don't remind me," she drawled before leaning back against the sofa.

Sean just laughed.

Montgomery closed her eyes and massaged her forehead with her fingertips. "Think, think, Go-Go. Think," she said.

Sean eyed her profile. "Go-Go?" he asked.

Montgomery opened one eye to side eye him. "It's my father's nickname for me," she explained.

"It fits," he said. "Can I call you that, Go-Go?"

She sat up and locked eyes with him. "Absolutely not. When you say it, it sounds like it means something else entirely," she said.

"True," he said with a wink.

Montgomery reclaimed her leaning position and

closed her eyes. "It's all about the spin," she said. "That's all. Spin it. Control it. Don't let it control you."

Sean furrowed his brows as he watched her give herself a pep talk.

"Okay," Montgomery said, sitting up straight again. "To beat back the frenzy of the press I'll secure an exclusive interview with *Celebrity Weekly*—they love you over there. I'll come up with a great backstory. We'll use the pictures from the photographer you hired. The *right* pictures."

"Ever the publicist," he said.

"Trust me, I've been working on presenting the right image my entire life," she said as she rose to her feet and crossed the space to scoop her phone up from the sofa where she had been sitting.

"Because of your father?" he asked. "That can't have been easy."

Montgomery looked up from her phone. "But it was fun," she said with a smile that was sad. "In those moments where I stole away and was fully me without him watching and judging and expecting... it was so much fun."

Both of their cell phones began to ring.

Sean looked down at his on the seat beside him. It was his mother.

And here we go.

Unlike himself, the majority of the Cress family hated the press, but kept on top of it nonetheless.

"My father," Montgomery said, tossing the phone back down onto the seat of the sofa.

Sean eyed her. She looked concerned.

Gone was the confident and in-charge woman he

had come to know. As she sat there fretting like a child caught being naughty by their parent, Montgomery had revealed yet another side to her. He now understood it was her concern for her father's opinion of her that she got married to keep from being judged by him.

Sean sent his mother to voice mail.

"You want to deal with your father now?" he replied. "Or in person?"

Montgomery shook her head as she bit at her bottom lip. She rose to start pacing as she made calls to secure the interview and tackling the blowout from the news of their elopement. The shift from nervous daughter to confident boss was intriguing.

Which one is the truest version of her?

Montgomery released a long sigh as she sat on the seat next to Sean again. "My father has been calling back-to-back-to-back," she said, sounding weary. "I love my dad, but his energy just drains me sometimes. He never takes off the clergy robe. *Never.*"

"However you want to handle this is fine with me," he assured her.

With a shake of her head, she picked up her phone.

When she moved to walk away, he reached for her wrist to keep her beside him.

"Montgomery!" her father exclaimed. "What is the mess on the news about you getting married in Vegas? Is that true?"

"Hi, Daddy," she said.

"Answer me, Montgomery Elise Morgan!" her father roared.

"Yes, I got married last night—"

"Have you lost your mind!" Reverend Morgan yelled.

Montgomery held the phone away from her ear.

Sean winced. He could only imagine the size of a man with a voice so deep.

"I understand that our decision to elope caught you by surprise," she said.

"This is completely unacceptable, Montgomery!" the man exclaimed.

She sighed.

"I am disappointed in you," Reverend Morgan said. "And I am confused at your behavior. This not who I raised you to be. Honor thy father and thy mother—"

Enough.

Sean eased the phone from Montgomery's hand and placed the call on speaker. "Hello, Reverend Morgan," he said.

The line went silent.

"I'm Sean Cress, Montgomery's husband—"

"I have *nothing* to say to a man who doesn't have the respect for himself or for me to meet me before marrying my daughter."

Sean made a mock face of horror.

Montgomery actually smiled a bit.

"Well, let's correct that," Sean said, keeping his voice affable. "But we'll give you whatever time you need to adjust to the news because I understand that it can be hard to accept that your daughter is now an adult able to make decisions for herself—come what may."

"Listen here—"

"And I get that in the heat of the moment—after

hearing that she made a decision as a grown woman, living on her own and running a successful business—that it might feel easier to choose your anger over her happiness," Sean said smoothly. "Parenting is tough—when they're kids, but once they're grown it *can* be easier. You've done your job to get her to adulthood so the training wheels needed in childhood can come off."

Montgomery's mouth and eyes opened wide.

The line went silent.

"If she does stumble and fall you can be there to support her through a life lesson," Sean continued. "But if she soars you choose to be happy for her."

"The nerve," Reverend Morgan muttered.

"I know for me, as her husband, I put Montgomery's feelings first," he said. "I'm sure as her father you do, too. Right?"

"I will not be disrespected by you or my daughter," her father continued, his voice hard and cold.

"*No one* wants to be disrespected, sir."

The line went silent again.

"She's happy, sir. At least I think she is—or she was," he added, looking to lock eyes with her.

Montgomery surprised him by leaning in close to the phone. "I am. I'm happy, Daddy," she said, her voice soft. "Please don't ruin it."

Does she mean that? Is she happy?

Sean reached to squeeze her hand, thinking it was the first time she spoke up for herself with her father. He felt proud of her for that.

"Take all the time you need," Sean said. "And I

look forward to finally meeting you and sharing some more good news—"

The call ended.

Sean handed Montgomery back her phone.

"I miss alcohol," she said before pressing a hand to her stomach.

"He'll get over it. Don't give up on him—"

"What if he gives up on me?" she asked.

"Then the foundation was shaky anyway, Montgomery," he told her.

She nodded in agreement. "And what about your parents?" she asked.

"Don't remind me," he drawled.

Upon their arrival in New York, they deboarded the plane and crossed the tarmac to his awaiting SUV. The cold winds whipped about them as snow began to fall. He was thankful to reach the vehicle.

"Colin," Sean said in greeting.

Montgomery gave the man a warm smile before taking the rear seat.

"Welcome home, Mr. and *Mrs.* Cress," Colin said with a wink before securely closing the door after Sean followed his wife's lead.

"Where are we headed, sir?" Colin asked, now in the driver's seat.

Sean looked over at Montgomery. She was looking out the window as she twisted her wedding rings on her finger. "Honey lover baby sugar," he said lightly.

She turned her head. "Huh?" she asked.

"Colin needs your address and I guess…so do I," he said.

"Right," she said. "It's 22 Belladonna Lane in Passion Grove, New Jersey."

"Got it," Colin said, typing the address into the GPS.

"*Belladonna* means beautiful lady in Italian," Sean offered.

"You speak Italian, too?" she exclaimed, turning on the seat to eye him.

Colin turned on his seat as well, looking back at them. "Excuse me, but do you two *know* each other?" he asked with a doubtful expression that was comical.

Sean and Montgomery faced forward to eye him and then looked at each other before breaking out in laughter. It was hard not to.

With a shake of his head, Colin turned on his seat and accelerated the vehicle forward to take the couple home.

Montgomery removed her tortoiseshell readers as she sat behind her desk in her home office. The sound of Duke Ellington and John Coltrane's "A Sentimental Mood" played from downstairs. She rolled her chair over to the window to see her vehicle parked in front of the house.

He's back.

Sean had dismissed Colin for the night and then driven her Jaguar to Passion Grove's small main street to grocery shop. She rose from her seat and crept over to the open door to listen to the sounds of him moving about the kitchen as he hummed to the popular jazz tune that had her feeling melancholy.

"You there, boss?"

Montgomery forgot she had been on the phone with her assistant. She walked back over to her desk. "Yeah, I'm here," she said, reclaiming her seat and replacing her glasses.

"I just sent the clip," Hanna said.

Montgomery opened the link in the email. She looked on at the video of Colin stopping the SUV at the end of the curved driveway where a small crowd of paparazzi was gathered in the street in front of her house. Thankfully, the oncoming winter storm had kept the crowd small. Sean lowered the rear window, revealing them together.

"Y'all look good together, boss," Hanna said via speakerphone.

Yes, we do.

She looked on as Sean flashed his winning smile. "We thank you for your interest in our marriage but we ask for privacy at this time and look forward to you learning more about our love story in our exclusive interview with *Celebrity Weekly* magazine," Sean said as scripted. "Now, get out of this weather. Be safe."

As questions flew at them, Montgomery and Sean gave a friendly wave before Sean raised the tinted window. Colin drove them up the drive where the press knew they were not allowed on private property.

The video ended.

They looked in love and happy.

And none of it was real.

"Thanks, Hanna," Montgomery said, reaching to end the call.

"Enjoy your night, boss. The weather is supposed to get really bad," Hanna said.

"Tell everyone to head home early. Be safe," she said.

"Done deal."

Montgomery replayed the video on mute and paused it at the sight of her and Sean smiling from the rear seat.

Earlier, the way he smoothly handled her father had made her feel relief because what she wanted with her father was an adult relationship with mutual respect. She had texted him earlier to say she loved him and he never responded. He was upset about the husband, but he would've been apoplectic about her getting pregnant before marriage.

Hell, I'm still dealing with it myself.

She tapped the touch screen of her computer to pull up her vision board. On it was her ideal life including her dream wedding dress, engagement ring, vacation spot and list of things that made a man *her* Mr. Perfect.

"Loving—of me and God. Attractive. Mature. Faithful. Gainfully employed. Attentive. Loyal. Handy around the house. Great lover. Traveler. Doesn't complain. No bad breath. Good health. Doesn't argue. Doesn't use profanity. Doesn't drink. Never been married. No children," Montgomery read before pausing.

She frowned a bit. She had only made it midlist.

It's a little lengthy.

"No children," she repeated.

How could she expect that from her future husband when she no longer could offer him the same?

She closed the vision board and focused on finishing a press release for a bestselling author and reading through incoming reviews for the debut album of a new indie recording artist whose single was trending on TikTok. By the time she shut down work for the day the skies were dark and the snow was falling heavily.

She texted her father to be safe in the weather but again he didn't respond, although she could see that he'd read it. She hated the guilt she felt at his anger. It nagged at her. She wasn't used to letting her father down. To being less than perfect in his eyes.

It was clear he wasn't dealing with her fall from grace, either.

Montgomery left the office and went down the stairs. She paused at the sight of the fireplace lit and the lights dimmed. She made her way around the corner to the hall leading to the kitchen. She leaned against the wall and watched Sean moving about her kitchen that she upgraded with new appliances and paint but was still in need of the walls being removed to increase its size and create an open floorplan.

Sean was so lost in his tasks that he didn't notice her standing there watching him.

He was just as intense in his cooking as he was in his lovemaking.

Wait. Don't move. Don't make me cum. Not yet. Please.

Montgomery bit the inside of her cheek and crossed her arms over her chest as her body pulsed to life at the memory of Sean's heated words. Earlier, when they first arrived to the house, as she showed him around the space and to the bedroom he would stay in, she had felt so nervous. Brushing past each other in the hall or innocent touches had stirred her. The man's presence wreaked havoc on her peace, and Montgomery had fled to her office to get some relief from her desire, afraid she would grab him and strip away every bit of his clothing.

I wish he had kissed me.

All night in Vegas as they enjoyed dinner and then focused on work, she had constantly wondered why he hadn't taken the chance to kiss her again. And she had to face why it bothered her that he hadn't.

I want Sean Cress.

To kiss.

To taste.

To feel.

To have inside me.

She enjoyed his flirtations. It was flattering. And arousing.

And now they were living together.

I did not think this through on so many, many levels.

Sean looked up from chopping green onion. He did a double take at her standing there and then smiled. "Hungry?" he asked. "With the winter storm coming I thought a pot of stew would work for dinner."

Montgomery pushed off the wall and came around the counter to stand beside him as he removed the lid of a large black ceramic stockpot she didn't recognize. "That's new?" she asked, tapping a fingernail against the side of the pot.

"Yes. That gourmet grocery store on Main Street is amazing," he said. "And you needed new pots. Yours were…"

Montgomery arched a brow and waited for him to finish his thought.

"Thin," he said.

The nerve. It's true, but damn.

"I don't really cook," she said. "Food delivery apps are my friend."

"I'll try to cook as much as I can when I'm not traveling for work—"

"Or attending the newest movie premieres, A-list parties, or appearances on celebrity gameshows," she added.

"Really keeping up with my life?" he asked, looking amused.

Montgomery cleared her throat, feeling embarrassed at what she just revealed. "I'm your publicist. Remember?" she said as she moved back around the counter to put space in between them.

"Right," he said, drawing it out and teasing her in the process before he chuckled.

"What's for dinner?" she asked.

"Beer-braised oxtail stew with my brother Lucas's version of bacon, chive and cheese biscuits," he said. "Sound good?"

"Sounds delicious," she said, hoping her stomach didn't rumble loud enough for him to hear.

"Wanna try it?" he asked, reaching for a tablespoon to scoop some of the stew.

Montgomery leaned across the counter as Sean fed her. She chewed. The meat was so tender and well seasoned. "Give me more," she said with a grunt of pleasure.

They both stiffened and shared a look.

The sound of their mingled cries of passion on that elevator echoed in her head.

She was the first to look away. To resist and ignore their desire for each other.

One day down and three hundred and sixty-four more to go. God help me.

Sean focused on rolling out the dough for the biscuits.

"Have you talked to your family?" she asked.

"My brothers? Yes. My parents? Not yet," he said.

"And your brothers?" she asked, thinking of the call from Monica that she didn't answer.

"Shocked," he said, grabbing a handful of flour from a large bowl—also new—to lightly dust the top of the dough.

"Because?"

"I never wanted to get married," Sean said.

"Because," she pressed.

Sean glanced up at her. "I enjoy my freedom. I like my life," he admitted.

See? Not the marrying type. But here we are married.

"You? Did you want to get married?" he asked.

Montgomery paused. "Yeah, I did. I had it all figured out and then…"

"And then we got stuck on that elevator," he finished for her.

She nodded, covering her face with her hand. "I still can't believe—"

"How good it was?" he asked, using a new biscuit cutter on the dough before placing each piece on a parchment-lined baking pan.

God, yes.

"That I had sex with an acquaintance," she said. "Maybe I have lost my mind. Maybe *we* lost our minds."

Sean picked up his phone and looked at the screen. "With the time zones we did not make twenty-four hours," he said.

"No, we're in it now and I'm not ready to return you just yet," she said playfully.

"Thanks," he drawled.

"It's just we haven't really talked about the future," she said. "The marriage has an end date, but not the baby. Where are we on childrearing? School? Visitation? Financial contributions? Everything is so out of order! It should be A-B-C not A-1-Z-B-square or whatever."

Sean slid the sheet pan into the oven and removed another with a batch of biscuits perfectly browned. "Then let's talk," he said.

The lights flickered.

Montgomery went still.

"Maybe we should check on the weather," Sean suggested, looking around the kitchen. "Where's the TV in here?"

Montgomery eyed him in disbelief. "You cannot be *that* privileged?" she said. "If so, you on the *wrong* side of Passion Grove, Richie Rich."

"Ha-ha," he said, coming around the counter and striding past her to leave the kitchen.

She turned and leaned back against the edge of the counter as she watched his tall and fit frame. He moved with confidence, strength and the swagger of a man who knew he had good d—

The lights flickered again.

And then went out.

"Oh, *hell* no!" Montgomery wailed in the darkness.

Light illuminated from the living room before Sean appeared in the hall, carrying his phone with its flashlight leading the way.

"You okay?" he asked.

She nodded. "Yeah," she said. "We are always stuck in emergencies together. Are we cursed?"

"Most definitely," Sean said without hesitation. "Do you have any candles?"

"Candles didn't make the shopping list?" she asked with a bit of snark.

"Petty much?" he asked.

"There's some in the hall closet," she said.

Sean reached for her hand and held it. "Come on," he said.

She followed behind him ever aware of just how warm his hand felt against hers. They reached the closet and worked together to light the fireplace, then lit candles and placed them on the counter in the kitchen and in the living room.

"Let there be light," Montgomery said, walking over to the front window to look out at the snow now inches high on the ground with more falling.

Sean came to stand beside her. "Looks like we might get snowed in," he said.

Montgomery raised her head to look at the snowflakes swirling around the tip of the lantern out on the street. "It's beautiful," she said.

In their reflection in the window, she watched as Sean slid his hands inside the pockets of his cords. "To me, I see aggravation," he said. "It will become dirty. Cause accidents. And slow down everything."

Montgomery feasted on his handsome features in the glass. "Who will our kid take after?" she asked.

He looked down at her.

She didn't dare look up at him.

"Whoever he or she wants to be," Sean said. "No pressure to make either of us so happy that he has to pretend to be what we want."

She did glance up at him then. "Like me?" she asked.

"Listen, my parents aren't much better than your dad," Sean admitted. "We all left our successful chef positions behind to take executive positions in the company they created because it's what they wanted. We all made a success of it, but in truth we set aside our own dreams to help theirs grow."

"But I thought you wanted to be the new CEO?" she asked.

"I do, but mainly to get my ideas put through," he admitted. "And…"

His words faded.

"And what?" she asked, surprised by the conflict she saw in the depths of his eyes.

"I feel it's owed to me, to be honest," Sean admitted. "I do the same corporate work as my brothers *and* maintain a full schedule taping three shows a year that help build the Cress, INC. brand name. I am the hardest working of the Cress brothers. I am always working or thinking about working. So it bugs me when they berate me for my fame and think I'm ego tripping, but I use that fame to help promote the family business. I am more than just a pretty face and great body."

Montgomery arched a brow. "Did you really just say that?" she mused with a bit of a smile.

"What? Too much?" he asked, nonplussed.

She couldn't tell if he was serious or not and gave him a judging look.

Sean just shrugged one broad shoulder.

He's adorable.

"Should we eat while we wait out the storm?" he asked, picking up a candle before turning to cross the living room.

"Might as well. There's nothing else to do," she said, following behind him.

Sean suddenly stopped.

Montgomery walked into the back of him and felt nothing but strength.

"Oh, there's something else we can do," he said, looking back at her over his shoulder.

Montgomery visibly swallowed.

Sean turned. "We haven't spent one night in this house and this thing between us is already bouncing off the walls—just like in the elevator," he said.

"Except there's more walls," Montgomery whispered before releasing a little shriek of pure frustration.

Sexual tension was being stoked without them even trying. It was organic and pure.

And hard to deny.

So very hard.

"I suggest a caveat to our prior agreement—a healthy sex life," he said, his voice deep and serious as his eyes searched hers by the light of the candles and the lit fireplace.

Montgomery thought of their steamy encounter and was intrigued to have another taste of him.

"No promises. No expectations. Full steam ahead with the divorce in a year," he added. "But in the meantime, we enjoy the one thing that brought us together in the first place. Amazing sex."

Montgomery took a step back from him and all the intense pleasure he dangled before her.

Sean watched the move. "Why fight it?" he asked.

Because I might not want the sex to ever end.

"Listen, it's your choice. Think it over. Let me know. My bedroom door is open," he said. "Because I want you in a way that distracts me."

Same.

Giving in would be so easy.

And he would be so hard.

Montgomery released a grunt.

But he is not my Mr. Perfect. Far from it.

Sean's expression became curious as he watched her.

But this isn't about my happily-ever-after.

Montgomery forced a smile she was afraid looked freakish when he frowned.

She stopped smiling. "Sean, I can't," she said.

Why waste time when I know we're not meant for each other?

He nodded in understanding. "It's up to you, Montgomery," he repeated before turning to make his way to the kitchen.

Give me more, Sean.

Montgomery went from begging for *it* to running away from *it*, when she knew she desperately ached for *it*.

To touch.

To stroke.

To taste.

To ride.

Saying yes would be easy. It's denying myself that's so very hard.

Six

Sean stood at the window of his bedroom at Montgomery's house, looking out at the snow continuing to heavily fall. Two tall and fat candles by his bedside gave the room a soft glow but it was the phone that lit upon his face as he looked at his parents on the screen. His father had been released from the hospital and they were in the movie theater at the townhouse.

"Look, husband, our son has remembered we exist," Nicolette said, her annoyance seeming to deepen her French accent. "Since we didn't get an invite to the wedding and weren't told he was marrying The Pretty Publicist."

"All done, *Maman*?" Sean asked.

"All done? I've only just begun," she snapped, her blue eyes blazing with angry fire..

"With?" he asked.

"With trying to figure out at just what point did you lose your mind? Do you even have a prenup? Just when did you decide marriage was for you because you have never shown a desire to be locked down as you say. I am confused by the decision, Sean."

"Montgomery changed my mind," he said, knowing it was a half-truth.

Nicolette paused, surprised by his answer.

"Dad?" Sean asked, giving him a chance to have his say as he eyed his father frowning as he sipped some steaming brew from a cup.

Phillip Senior cut his eyes up. "Prenup?" he asked before taking a sip that brought on a swear as he frowned some more.

"Yes—at Montgomery's suggestion," Sean assured him.

"Good. Right now I'm more concerned with what *is* this?" he asked, his English accent clipping his words.

"Seaweed tea," Nicolette said. "It gives you energy, immunity and a healthy heart."

"Bloody late for *that*," Phillip Senior snarked.

His mother patted his father's cheek and blew him a soft kiss before turning to eye Sean.

"Où est exactement votre nouvelle épouse?" Nicolette asked.

"Asleep." Sean answered her question of where exactly was his new bride.

Phillip Senior chuckled and raised his cup to him in toast. "A Cress man through and through," he said.

Anything but because Montgomery offered to be

my wife in this marriage of convenience but does not want to be my lover.

"I'm ready to go to bed," his father said, his voice showing his fatigue.

It would take six to eight weeks for him to fully regain his strength and heal the wound on his breast-plate from the surgery.

"As soon as the weather permits, I'll be by the townhouse to collect my things and check on you," Sean said.

"Bring the new Mrs. Cress," Nicolette said.

"If you agree to surrender the fight and not corner her with one of your bullying sessions," Sean said, well aware that his mother had tried to scare off each of the wives or girlfriends of his brothers. "Besides, your stunt doesn't seem to work."

Nicolette made a face of distaste that amused him.

Raquel, Monica, Jillian and Bobbie were each officially a Mrs. Cress.

"One day when you become a parent you will understand my motivations, Sean Pierre Cress," Nicolette told him.

That will be sooner than you think.

He was surprised at his desire to tell them the news but stuck to his agreement with Montgomery to keep the news until they were in their second trimester.

"Bonsoir," he said, wishing them a good night in French.

"Bonsoir," they said in return.

He ended the call and tossed the phone onto the middle of the bed. As he turned from the chill of standing near the windows in need of upgrading, Sean noticed cold permeated the entire room. With a frown he rubbed his bare arms and walked over to press his hand to the radiator. It was frigid.

The heat is off, too.

The thin cotton sleep pants he wore did nothing to shield him, but his thoughts went to Montgomery. He hurried to grab his phone to turn on the flashlight before blowing out the candles and crossing the carpeted floor to fling the door open and rush down the hall to her bedroom. It was dark but his light showed Montgomery was in the middle of her bed, huddled under the covers and curled into a ball.

His heart pounded as he went to her side to ease back the comforter. She was asleep but shivering from the cold. "Montgomery," he said, gently nudging her shoulder to awaken her.

He noticed that her lush lashes were naturally fuller at the outer corners as she blinked before opening them to look up at him. "Hey," he said.

Such beautiful eyes.

"It's cold," she said, resembling a turtle as she ducked her head back under the covers as if it was a shell.

"The heat went out," he said, reaching to gather her and her bedcovers into his arms to lift with ease.

"That damn boiler," she muttered, snuggling her face against his neck.

Sean's body reacted to that as he used his phone to guide them out of the room, out to the hall and down the stairs. He felt her trembles and they reminded him of the feel of her when they climaxed together.

It feels good to hold her.

When they reached the living room, he regretted having to place her on the sofa. "Hold tight," he said.

"Okay," she said, sounding as if her teeth chattered.

He moved over to the fireplace to relight the wood stacked inside it.

After they ate an early dinner by the fire and decided to go to bed, he had doused the fire to ensure safety. Now they needed it badly to fight off the frigid cold created by the winter storm still raging outdoors. Soon the crackle of fire echoed. He moved the coffee table from in front of the sofa and then pushed the furniture forward to be closer to the heat before he lay down on the sofa under the covers beside her.

She was still trembling as he gathered her close with his head atop her head. He was surprised—and pleased—when she didn't protest.

"Still love the winter?" he asked.

"N-n-n-no," she stammered.

Sean chuckled.

The side of Montgomery's face lay against Sean's chest and the sound of his chuckle that seemed a second nature to him was deep. The light spray of flat hairs on his chest was soft. His muscles hard.

And the smell of him.

Something warm with woody notes.

She fought the natural urge to ease one of her legs atop his. Or to let the hand lightly resting on his muscled arm slide down to slip beneath the elastic waistband of his pajama bottoms.

Why fight it?

"Are you warming up?" Sean asked.

Am I.

Her body was on high alert from being pressed against him. Everything either throbbed or raced. One of his brown nipples was in her line of vision and she wanted so desperately to trace it with her tongue. Until it hardened. And he moaned in pleasure.

"Try to get some rest," he said, sounding as if his own voice was heavy with oncoming sleep.

When he pressed a kiss to the top of her head it felt the most natural thing in the world.

She stared into the embers of the fireplace, imagining giving in to her desires, until soon her eyes closed as she drifted to sleep as well.

Montgomery was awakened as her body was jostled. "Huh?" she asked, raising her head from Sean's chest.

"I didn't mean to wake you," he said as she looked up at him. "I was getting up."

Their eyes locked.

"Why?" she asked, still half-asleep and wondering just how much time had passed.

"Because I am a man with only so much control, Montgomery," he said, notching his chin up a bit.

She turned her head and looked down to find him aroused and his inches standing tall against the comforter. "Ooh," she said as the core of her womanhood pulsed to life—like it applauded him.

It's up to you, Montgomery, Sean had said.

"Sorry. I was trying to get up before—"

She reached her hand inside his pants and gripped him with a deep moan from the back of her throat.

It was his time to tremble.

"Montgomery," he warned, his voice strained.

"It's up to me. Remember?" she said, looking up at him and loving the heat in his eyes. "New deal?"

"Name it," he said.

"We can add sex to our marriage but I need fidelity," she said as she began to stroke his hard inches from root to tip. Slowly. "No scandals. No mistresses. Deal?"

"Deal," he answered firmly as he placed his hands under her arms to drag her body atop his.

Her face was above his. In his eyes she saw the flickering embers of the fireplace mixed with his hunger. She felt the thundering beat of his heart. And his hard inches pressed against her belly. "I'm serious, Sean," she stressed, her eyes searching his.

"So am I," he promised just before he raised his head to capture her mouth with his own.

Montgomery's moan was filled with hunger as she gave in. Fully.

Their kiss was slow and sensual. Meant to heighten their desires. To tease with promise for more.

She pushed the cover to the floor beside the sofa and brought her knees up to rest on either side of his body, pressing the length of his hardness against her core. With a grunt she rolled her hips.

"Yes," Sean moaned into her mouth as he brought his hands beneath the satiny gown she wore to grip her buttocks.

She gasped at his heated touch, ending their kiss with a lick of his mouth and soft suck of his bottom lip before sitting up with her hands pressed to his chest.

He eyed her in wonder as she gripped the edges of her gown to raise it over her head. She felt the heat of the flames in the fireplace against her nudity as she brought her hands up to cup her own breasts.

"Montgomery," Sean moaned.

"Huh?" she asked with a tease.

That door inside her where she succumbed to her passion was opened again. Just like that night they were trapped together in the elevator. It was a part of her she never knew existed. Where she found power in her sexuality. Where there was no shame or inhibition. No desire to be a "good girl" and present the image of perfection. Where she did not put the wishes of others ahead of her own. Be shy? Pretend?

No.

She raised her arms above her head.

"I love your body," Sean marveled. "I *love* it."

"Now we can see each other," she said.

"Damn right," he agreed.

She dipped down to suck one of his nipples to hardness before shifting over to do the same to the other.

He hissed in pleasure.

Montgomery lightly licked a trail down the hard ridges of his abdomen as she moved backward to sit atop his knees. With a look up at him, she freed his hardness from his sleep pants to stroke. His hips arched upward at her touch. She eyed the dark length of him and his thickness before stroking the smooth tip with her tongue.

Sean cried out.

She sucked him—slowly and deeply—enjoying the feel of him against her tongue.

His hands entwined in her hair.

She took in all of him until the soft hairs surrounding the root of his shaft tickled her lips and the scent of his soap filled her nose. With patience she continued to taste him by firelight, enjoying its heat as the one inside her rose. Just the sight of Sean's face twisted in pleasure fueled her.

"You like it?" she asked before giving his tip another lick.

"Too much," he said, easing her head back to free himself before he reached to pull her body up against his again.

He shifted them on their sides on the sofa. Facing each other. Eyes locked.

She raised one leg to drape over his hip as she settled her head atop one arm and gripped the strength of the other. The feel of his hardness was there between their bodies, reminding her that he was more than ready to fill her with it. The soft hairs on his chest teased her hard nipples, and Sean used his fingertip to softly trace her body from shoulder to thigh.

She took a deep inhale.

When he raised her leg to place it on his shoulder, she gripped his arm and rolled her hips as he softly stroked her pulsing bud. It danced for him and his eyes devoured the expressions of her face as he brought her to the edge of a slow but intense climax.

Yes. Yes. Yes. Yes!

The anticipation of her release made her ache.

"Do you want it?" he asked, his voice thick. "Do you want to cum?"

Her fingernails dug into his arm as she quivered. "Y-y-yes," she whispered.

Sean smiled and used the arm she lay on to grip her body and pull her closer to kiss her deeply as he did indeed make her climax. He swallowed her cries of pleasure and was relentless in massaging her bud as she shook from the white-hot spasms that controlled her.

And just when she thought she could take no more, Sean freed the bud and gripped his dark inches to guide his dick inside her tightness with a thrust of his hips.

Together they broke their heated kiss to release rough cries in the space between their open mouths. It blended with the crackle of the firewood.

Slowly, he stroked inside her as he gripped the soft flesh of her buttocks. She reached to do the same to him, enjoying the flex and release of his muscles with each thrust that pushed her into such a deep climax that she felt her inner walls clutch his inches. Again and again and again. A fine sheen of sweat coated their bodies as he quickened his pace.

"Sean," she gasped. "Don't stop. Don't stop."

He didn't.

Even once she was weak and sure she didn't have the strength or the will to walk, he held her tightly and continued his onslaught.

She felt his inches get harder—like steel—and his body stiffen. The look in his eyes changed in that moment just before he flung his head back and released a long roar that echoed. Gripping his face, she jerked his head forward and kissed him, seeking his tongue with her own to suckle it as she worked her inner walls to drain him of every bit of his release. She didn't stop until he was trembling, releasing small whimpers and spent.

"Damn," he whispered in the aftermath as he pressed kisses to her sweat-dampened face. "Damn."

Montgomery pressed her hands to his chest, feeling the hard pounding of his heart, and couldn't find one regret for the choice she made to have him. Not one.

Ding-dong. Ding-dong. Ding-dong.

Sean awakened from the steady ringing of the doorbell. Montgomery was still asleep where they lay on the floor atop a pallet he made from comforters and blankets. The intensity of the fire had died down and during the night they had snuggled closer for more warmth.

Being sure to cover her nudity with more blankets, Sean searched for his pajama bottoms to pull on and grabbed a throw cover to wrap around him. He was pleased to see the lights were back on as he made his way to the front door to ease it open. The winter winds still were brutal and circled around the tall and thin man standing there with a scowl on his face. "Good morning. Can I help you?" he said.

The man shook his head. "I guess you're my daughter's...*husband*," he said, his voice deep and filled with his annoyance.

Montgomery's father.

Sean stepped back and opened the door fully. "Yes, I am, Mr. Morgan. It's nice to meet you," he said, looking over at Montgomery still sleeping on the floor.

"*Reverend* Morgan," he corrected him, knocking snow off his boots before stepping inside. "You would know that had you bothered to meet me."

"I see neither time nor the cold has cooled you off yet," Sean said with a smile.

"And freezing in here all night didn't teach you any manners," the reverend countered.

"Let me wake up Montgomery."

"Don't," the man demanded as he crossed the living room. "I don't have anything to say to her. I just came to check on the boiler."

Sean followed behind him. "That's good of you considering you're not talking to her," he said as the man opened a door leading down into the basement.

"I want her to respect me, not suffer," he said before descending the stairs.

"Thank you for thinking of us," Sean offered, dodging a spider web that almost covered his face like a palm.

The reverend paused and looked back. "I said *her*," he said with emphasis before turning around.

"Sir," Sean said.

"Good start," Reverend Morgan drawled.

Why am I even trying?

Sean released a heavy breath.

For Montgomery. And this man will be the grandfather to my child.

"Sir," Sean repeated with emphasis. "I'm from a good family. I have a great career—"

"Oh. I *know* who you are," the man said before opening the electric panel on the wall to turn off the electricity.

"Great!" Sean exclaimed.

Reverend Morgan snorted in derision.

"Is that good or bad?" Sean asked. "Listen, the sex tape was from years ago—"

"The sex tape!" Reverend Morgan exclaimed, his voice booming against the walls.

Uh-oh.

Sean felt out of sorts. He had never met anyone who disliked him.

"Listen, Reverend Morgan, not speaking to Montgomery is—"

His temporary father-in-law was bent down near the boiler, but paused to look back over his shoulder at him. "Is what?"

"A move meant to make sure she does what you want instead of what she wants," Sean continued. "Whether you mean it to be or not, it's emotional blackmail. Sir."

Another grunt.

"Where was all this wisdom when you made a sex tape?" Reverend Morgan asked with snark. "Oh, wait. There was none."

Sean nodded. "As men we all make mistakes. No one is perfect...or should expect perfection," he finished.

Reverend Morgan waved his hand at him dismissively and focused on working on the boiler.

Sean hoisted the dragging blanket up higher on his shoulders to keep it off the floor as he looked around at the basement. It was unfinished, stacked with containers and had a slightly damp scent to it. When he thought of the finished basement at the Cress family townhome, complete with the housekeeper apartment, wine cellar, laundry room and storage, the space left a lot to be desired. There was size but no function.

At the sound of the metal gate of the boiler closing, Sean turned to find his father-in-law wiping his hands on a cloth he shoved back inside the overalls he wore under his leather winter coat.

"That boiler needs to be replaced, man of the house," Reverend Morgan said with sarcasm.

"No problem," Sean assured him.

The man breezed past him and climbed up the stairs. The scent of the heat rising in the radiators already began to fill the air.

"Reverend Morgan," he called up to him.

The man paused.

"I know it couldn't have been easy raising a daughter alone," Sean said. "Montgomery is proof you did a good job."

"And your recipe for Bolognese is salty," Reverend Morgan said sarcastically, leaving the basement and closing the door.

"What the—!" Sean said in indignation before taking off to climb the stairs two at a time, relieved the man hadn't locked the door.

He reached the living room just in time to see Reverend Morgan leave the house, closing the front door behind him. Not a second later Montgomery's head popped up from the floor. "Were you pretending to be asleep?" he asked her in astonishment as he crossed the room to stand beside their pallet.

Montgomery lay back down and rolled over onto her back to look up at him. "I knew it was my father at the door," she admitted. "I just swore he was coming to preach a sermon. Trust me, pretending to be asleep has gotten me out of a lot of *long* conversations."

Sean let the blanket around his shoulders fall to the floor. "Or you could have talked to him the same way I did," he said.

She sat up. "What did he say?"

"Same-o-same about respect," Sean told her. "And that one of my recipes was too salty. Can you believe that?"

Montgomery looked taken aback. "He said that?" she asked.

"Is he a fan of one of my shows?" Sean asked, sitting down on the sofa watching her think about the question.

"I don't know," she said. "I left home for college and never moved back. I don't know what my father does in his free time. I honestly don't know. I never thought about it."

"Montgomery, a part of your father seeing you as more than his little girl is you presenting yourself as more than that," Sean said.

She looked doubtful. "Easier said than done."

"I'm going to finally clean up the kitchen," he said, rising to his feet and ignoring the distraction of the covers having fallen down to her lap as she stared into the dying embers in the fireplace.

Seven

One month later

Montgomery sat behind her desk at the midtown Manhattan offices of Montgomery Morgan Publicity. She looked around at the modest offices housing her six-member team made up of two public relations specialists, her executive assistant, Hanna, an account manager, graphic designer and college intern. She took pride in her accomplishments and the success of the business she built from the ground up, starting her career as a college intern and working her way up through the ranks in positions at public relations departments at publishing houses, music companies, fashion designers and corporations. Twice she had been named on *Ebony's* Power 100 list and been featured in *Essence*.

It was quite a feat at just thirty-three.

But with every passing day, her focus was far less on her business.

She turned her clear office chair to look out the window. But it was not the view of the metropolis showing signs that winter was ending and spring was soon to begin that she enjoyed. It was her reflection against the glass as she pulled the turquoise dress she wore close around her belly swollen with Sean's child. Her days of being able to hide her pregnancy were drawing to an end.

With each kick and flutter of the baby's movement, every doctor's appointment that showcased a new milestone, every purchase in preparation of its arrival and the steady growth of her belly, her love for the baby grew and her fear of motherhood lessened.

She reached for her phone from atop the modern black L-shaped desk with bronze accent legs that matched the decor of the entire office suite. She pulled up her father's number and called him, hating how nervous she felt to reach out to her own father. After three weeks of attending church every Sunday and being ignored, Montgomery had stopped going. Still, every day she left a voice mail or text message hoping one day he would close the divide between them.

She needed to be forgiven.

For so long, she feared outright disobeying him but never had she imagined him cutting her out of his life completely. Not for getting married.

Her call went straight to voice mail. "Hey, Daddy. It's me. Montgomery. As always, I hope you're okay," she said, her voice shaky with her hurt. "I have some good news and I wanted you to be the first to know that Sean and I…are having a baby, Dad."

Sharp pain radiated across her chest and she pressed her eyes closed as tears threatened to fall. *Damn it.*

"You're going to be a grandfather," she said, her voice soft with her hurt. "I love you."

She ended the call and released a heavy breath.

Knock-knock.

Montgomery released the dress to billow about her frame again before she turned. "Yes, Hanna?" she asked at the sight of her assistant standing in the doorway holding an enlarged copy of the upcoming cover of *Celebrity Weekly.*

"This just arrived," Hanna said, wiggling her eyebrows as she crossed the room and set the posterboard atop her desk—and close to her boss's face.

Montgomery leaned back to take in the photo of herself and Sean posed together for their exclusive interview on the surprise nuptials. The photo was taken during the wedding ceremony.

The digital edition had been released online last week.

"Y'all look great together," Hanna said, still holding the corner of the large 16x20 foam board as she came around it.

We do.

She remembered the shot well. It was the moment just after they were pronounced husband and wife. The glow of the candlelight against the night views of

Vegas in the background was spectacular. Her dress truly seemed whimsical and romantic in the setting. The photo had quickly gone viral to rave reviews.

Her heart pounded a little as she leaned in to study her face. And the look in her eyes.

She gasped at the discovery.

There, in the brown depths of her feline-like eyes, was her hunger for his kiss. The one that landed on her cheek instead of her mouth, filling her with such disappointment.

Not that they hadn't made up for it.

She had lost count over the past four weeks how often one of them would leave their bedroom to seek out the other in theirs. Whether long, slow and sensual or fast and hard, they would get lost in each other for minutes or hours.

They would disagree over any and everything. And their lives were lived separately with them only making joint appearances for his family or a public event. There were even a few nights he would go out alone and return in the early hours of the morning. She never questioned him. She felt she had no right— even though she would wait up for his safe return in her bedroom without him knowing.

Between those sheets, nothing mattered but their pleasure.

Nothing at all.

With the hint of a smile, she tilted her head to the side and wrapped the end of her ponytail around her finger.

Just that morning, after being away for a week to tape a new special in the Swiss Alps, Sean returned and knocked on the door to the bathroom before peeking his head inside to ask to join her in the shower. She agreed and through the steam, she saw that he was naked. Without hesitation, she had pulled the curtain back and reached for his wrist to pull him under the spray of water with her.

As her body grew with their child, she assumed his desire for her would wane.

She was so very wrong.

She licked and bit down on her bottom lip, remembering the feel of his body lightly pounding against hers as he stroked inside her from behind as the water sprayed down against them, plastering her hair to her scalp and ruining her silk press.

Well worth it.

The man had climaxed twice with a rough cry as the muscles of his body tensed and his hardness pulsed with each shot of his release inside her.

She grunted at the electric memory.

As Hanna gave her an odd look, Montgomery cleared her throat and sat up straight to regain her cool and composed decorum as she almost figuratively melted in her chair.

Because of Sean Cress, she had added exquisite lover to her list for her Mr. Perfect. Although she wondered if there was anyone who could best him physically.

Perhaps love will give my future husband the upper hand.

Over the weeks they had developed a friendship and were comfortable with each other but theirs was no love match. Being with Sean had taught her that there could be great passion without love.

And it was that element she wanted in her life. Still.

A loving relationship with a man with whom she was compatible and had more in common than amazing sex.

Bzzzzzz. Bzzzzzz. Bzzzzzz.

Montgomery turned her phone over and her heart raced to see a photo of her father's face. "That's it for now, Hanna," she said, picking up the device to answer the call.

Hanna quickly left and closed the door behind her.

"Hi, Daddy," she said, letting her emotions swell in her voice and hoping he had set aside his anger at her. Finally. That he was able to just be happy for her.

"Congratulations, Go-Go," he said.

She closed her eyes and then pressed the bridge of her nose between her fingers. "Thank you," she said.

The line went silent.

"Daddy?" she said, not sure he was still on the line.

"I'm here," he said.

It felt so awkward. So forced.

Not what she hoped for. No joy. No excitement.

Her father's silence was just as heavy with his judgment as were his harsh words.

Montgomery pressed a hand to her belly, praying she had more forgiveness and grace in her for her child than her father had given her. "It's good to hear from you. Why don't you come over for dinner," she offered. "Sean can make some less salty Bolognese."

That did get a grunt.

Montgomery felt exasperated and clutched her free hand into a fist. But what surprised her above all was the desire she had to talk to Sean. He had proven himself able to lift her spirits by making her laugh or offering sound advice.

"Am I welcome back to church?" she asked.

"I never once said you weren't welcome, Montgomery," he said.

No, you made me feel unwelcomed—unwanted— and actions speak louder than words.

But she did not say that. She couldn't bring herself to do it. Old habits seemed hard for her to break.

Montgomery, a part of your father seeing you as more than his little girl is you presenting yourself as more than that.

Sean's words resonated.

"Daddy, can I call you back?" she asked, wanting freedom from his judgment.

"I expect to see you Sunday at church," he said, his voice demanding.

Montgomery held the phone from her face to stare down at it in shock. Anger at her father sparked in her. He denied her very presence in church and then made her feel like she was not justified in no longer attending.

What in the hell?

"Okay," she said, setting the phone down and letting her finger hover over the red button to end the call.

"Go-Go," he said.

"Yes?"

"Be safe," he said with more warmth than she had heard in his tone in months.

"I will, Dad," she said.

He ended the call.

Montgomery released a long sigh and leaned back against her chair with her eyes closed.

Bzzzzzz. Bzzzzzz. Bzzzzzz.

She opened one eye to look at her phone. With a shake of her head, she smiled at Sean's name on the screen. She reached to answer the call and placed it on speaker. "Mr. Cress, how may I assist you, sir?" she said, her hands splayed against her belly.

"Mr. Cress?" he asked, his deep voice amused. "I think I would like you to call me that next time I'm sexing you."

Her heart pounded. "Really?" she asked.

"Definitely," he countered.

Montgomery chuckled. "Mr. Cress, if you're nasty?" she asked, a play on the lyric from the Janet Jackson song "Nasty."

That made Sean laugh from his belly.

And she enjoyed doing that because his laughter was infectious.

"Listen, I'm still at the house and the lights went out," Sean said. "I had an electrician come out and the house needs massive rewiring."

Cha-ching. Cha-ching.

"What's the estimate?" she asked with a shake of her head. "And how soon can they repair it?"

"He's still working on that, but it's going to take close to a month to complete," Sean said.

Montgomery released a heavy breath. "I love my house, but it's becoming a money trap," she said.

Over the weeks she had shared with him her wishes on how to completely update the home to be a showcase again.

"Listen, we'll stay at my condo in Tribeca until all of the work is repaired and I'll pay the bill so don't worry about it," he said.

"No," she protested. "It's my home. My bill."

"And you're my wife," he stressed.

"For ten more months," she countered.

"I live there," he continued.

"For ten more months," she repeated.

"And staying at my condo? Can I offer that or does that offend your sensibilities as well?" he asked. "Or maybe you want to pay rent?"

"Is that sarcasm, Mr. America's Favorite Chef?" she asked.

"I'm nice, not perfect," he said.

At least not for me.

"You know I'm leaving next week for work and I would feel better making sure you are good before then, Montgomery," he said.

"But that's not your responsibility."

"Untrue. You are my wife—no matter the end date and you are pregnant with my child," he said. "That makes you my responsibility. I can't change who I am."

A wealthy playboy married to a woman he doesn't love.

"Listen, we have dinner tonight at my parents',"

he said. "We'll go by the condo first and you can see if you like it."

"Okay, Sean," she acquiesced, releasing the nervousness she had of stepping deeper into his world of wealth and luxury.

Sean looked out the apron window of his condo at the view of the waterfront in the Tribeca section of Manhattan. He considered this an investment property and a second home from the Cress family townhome. At times he allowed out-of-town guests to use it, threw parties, or found the solace unavailable in a family home. No one in the family except Lucas knew about his luxury hideaway in a building exclusive enough to draw the likes of other high-profile celebrities and athletes.

For Sean, being in a large, well-known family, and a frequent subject of the press meant having something that was just for him. His parties were legendary and Sean took great pleasure in having a part of his life not wrapped up in being a Cress.

He glanced back over his shoulder at Montgomery standing and looking up at one of the many large paintings of himself that he'd been gifted over the years by fans of his shows who were extremely talented. There were also many photos of himself with other celebrities and dignitaries—including a couple of presidents of the United States. It was also in the condo where he kept all of the awards he'd won over the years.

He eyed her profile, again struck by how beautiful

she was to him. He loved the way she had cleverly hidden her pregnancy from the world. Another secret.

One he felt himself get more excited about with each passing day.

The first time Montgomery grabbed his hands and pressed them to her belly as the baby kicked—or maybe even did flip-flops—his heart had burst with love for the baby. His child.

Our child.

He let his eyes enjoy the sight of her in the black ruffle trapeze dress she wore under a black satin tuxedo blazer with high heels. Time had not dulled his attraction to her. In fact, it was stronger. He couldn't get enough of her. And when he would go to her bedroom seeking the pleasure he craved, she never denied him. Whether sleeping, working or reading, she would welcome him into her bed. For him, there was nothing better than being awakened from his sleep by Montgomery climbing into his bed beside him, naked and ready.

But it was more than just her body.

Montgomery Morgan—she hadn't changed her name—was intelligent and witty when she wasn't hiding behind one of her facades—cold and formal for business; innocent and fragile for her father.

Suddenly, Montgomery looked over at him with a smile, with her ebony hair in loose curls pulled back from her face with a thin elastic band with a crystal adornment that rested just above her ear. His gut clenched.

"Will our child have its father's ego?" she mused,

walking over to stand beside him. "Because *this* is a shrine. And clearly a bachelor pad."

Sean chuckled as he looked around at the sleek and modern decor in black and charcoal. There was no softness to be found. It was the space of a man. "We'll only be here until the house is ready," he reminded her.

"It's a beautiful space," she said, looking out at the view of the water as the sun began to lower. "Well worth every million, I'm sure."

Sean didn't miss the hint of contention in her voice. It was there any time his wealth came up. The elephant in the room he chose not to address. He wasn't a classist, but he couldn't pretend he didn't enjoy the trappings of wealth. And just by the very existence of their child, he or she would automatically become an heir to both the Cress family fortune and the prosperity he had garnered in his own right.

"There's a pool, spa and library in the building," he shared, easing his hands into the pockets of the black suit he wore. "Security, doorman and concierge."

She looked up at him. "Stop selling me, Sean," she said. "Thank you for letting me stay here while my house is being worked on. I promise I'm not ungrateful."

He bent his head to press a kiss to her forehead.

Her gasp was crystal clear.

He looked down at her eyes finding the same surprise he felt at the tender gesture.

I couldn't help myself.

"Ready?" he asked, stepping away from her.

"To tell your family I'm pregnant?" she asked, the

click of her high heels indicating she followed behind him to the door. "Definitely not."

Sean opened the front door and held it for her. "They're not that bad," he insisted.

Montgomery gave him a look as she passed him out into the hall. "Just keep an eye on your mother," she requested. "I heard she likes to corner newbies."

True.

It really was a trait he wished his mother would stop. Although he was sure she was just being a mother bear to her cubs, he knew the optics were not great. Serving as a gatekeeper to their family barked of elitism.

"To be fair, I didn't hold back giving your father my opinion of how he treats you, so feel free to politely put her in her place," he said.

Montgomery looked surprised. "What did you say?" she asked as he closed the door and pressed his thumb to the biometric lock to secure it.

"Huh?" he asked as they walked down the ornate hall to the elevator.

"What did you say to my father?" she asked.

"That whether he meant to or not, the way he was treating you was emotional blackmail," he told her with a shrug of his shoulder. "It's a way to control someone. Do what I say or I will withdraw my love, my attention, my support."

Montgomery frowned.

"Did I overstep?" he asked.

She shook her head. "No. I just never looked at it like that and I wish it wasn't true," she said, her sadness so evident as she looked down at her feet in deep thought.

"Hey, hey, hey," he said, placing his hand to her chin to raise her head. "You guys talked today. Right? Things are beginning to thaw with you and your dad. It will get better."

She gave him a smile that was forced.

As Sean drove them to his parents' townhouse in his Bentley Continental, he noticed Montgomery remained silent as she looked out the window. He found his eyes kept going to her and he had to fight not to reach for her hand just to assure her. Comfort her. Be there for her.

And when he thought he saw the glimmer of a tear on her cheek, Sean did reach across the seat to take her hand into his own. She instantly squeezed it with her fingers and looked over at him with a soft smile of thanks.

At the townhouse, after Sean parked on the street outside the home and helped Montgomery out of the vehicle, she paused on the street to look up at the towering Victorian-era structure. It was impressive, particularly during the inky night, and the up-lighting made it seem like a beacon in the darkness. His eyes studied her face, looking for more of her unspoken disdain for affluence, but she just smiled at him as he opened the gate of the wrought iron fence lining the front of the property and they climbed the steps together.

"Careful in those heels," he said, feeling protective.

"I could outrun you in these," she said with confidence.

"All I ask is you wear them later—with nothing

else on," he said as they reached the top step and he pressed the doorbell.

The door opened, not giving her a chance to answer, although he caught the light of interest spark in her eyes.

"Good evening, Mr. and Mrs. Cress," Felice the housekeeper said, stepping back to hold the door for them.

"How are you doing, Felice?" he asked, giving her a warm smile.

The middle-aged woman gave him a wink. "Better now that my favorite is back home—for a little while anyway," she said.

Sean clasped his hands and laughed. "Good to see you, too, Felice," he said.

"Charmer," Montgomery whispered to him after they passed the woman, crossed the marbled entryway and then stepped through the open foyer door into the living room.

"Here are the newlyweds," Nicolette said with a large smile from her seat on the sofa beside his father.

Sean creased his brow at his mother's insincerity. She wasn't acting for a performance, just politeness. But that was Nicolette. To anyone outside of their inner circle, life was grand and there were no worries. He didn't doubt that keeping up appearances had her nerves stretched thin.

"Hello, everyone," Montgomery said as Felice took their coats.

With his wife at his side, Sean made the rounds. The entire family was in attendance. Lincoln and Bobbie, Phillip Junior and Raquel, Gabriel and Monica, Coleman and Jillian, and Lucas—the lone unmarried Cress brother.

"Where are my nieces?" Sean asked as he accepted the snifter of thirty-year-old brandy from Phillip Junior.

"In the nursery with the au pair we hired for the night," Nicolette said, her hand clasping his father's knee. "I'm giving my daughters-in-law a little respite for a few hours while we celebrate my love getting a good checkup at the cardiologist."

Phillip Senior turned up his lips at the soda water he was drinking as he eyed the liquor his sons were sipping.

"What's your drink, Montgomery?" Phillip Junior asked.

"I have it, Mr. Phillip," Felice said as she entered the room carrying a tray and walked up to Montgomery sitting with his sisters-in-law—completely fitting in. "Mr. Sean asked for Chef to be sure to have this for you whenever you visit."

Over the rim of his glass, Sean watched Montgomery's surprise at her favorite drink, pear-flavored sparkling water topped with fresh slices of the fruit.

She looked over at him across the living room and mouthed, "Thank you."

"My sons are in love," Nicolette said, her eyes slightly reserved. "All of you are staring at your wives."

Sean looked around him and it was indeed true.

Lincoln eyed Bobbie and her wild mane of loose curls.

Phillip Junior was taking in the length of Raquel's leg exposed by the slit in her dress.

Gabriel seemed intrigued by Monica innocently stroking the base of her throat as she talked to the other women.

Coleman had just motioned for Jillian with an incline of his head toward the kitchen.

Unlike his brothers, his marriage to Montgomery was no love match and, at that moment, he was well aware that they believed it to be.

More deception.

"My turn is coming," Lucas assured them.

All the brothers reached to give him light and playful punches. Although Lucas was thirty years of age, he was undeniably the baby of the family.

"Je ne suis pas pressé, mon petit garçon," Nicolette said, telling him she was in no rush, my baby boy.

Lincoln, their half brother whom they had come to love, chuckled as the other Cress brothers threw their hands up in exasperation at their mother's insistence on babying a grown man.

Lucas just shrugged and looked pleased because he knew being the "favorite" was a playful bone of contention with his brothers.

Montgomery excused herself and walked over to him, lightly touching his arm. "Can we go up and see the children?" she asked.

He finished his drink and handed his glass to Phillip Junior "Sure. And I'll show you my old room," he said, taking her hand in his and leading her down the hall and into the bustling kitchen.

"Wait," he said, stopping before they reached the elevator in the corner. "You okay with this?"

"I use them at work all the time," she said. "Plus, in the end, I wasn't scared anymore. Remember?"

More, Sean. Give me more.

"Oh, I remember," he said as they continued to the elevator.

"Your mother hasn't said much to me," she said as soon as he closed the gate and pressed the button for the fifth floor.

"I thought you wanted her to keep her distance?" he asked.

"I do," she said, playing with her ear.

Something she did when she was nervous.

"No worries, Montgomery," he said as the elevator slid to a stop.

They crossed the massive den to reach the nursery. The au pair held a finger to her mouth from where she sat rocking Emme to point to Collie, who was snuggled under the covers in the middle of the bed with her mouth open and her glasses on the bedside table as she slept.

Montgomery continued forward to quietly look down at the baby—now three months old.

"Would you like to hold her?" the au pair asked with the hint of a German accent.

"Yes," she stressed.

Sean remained near the door and looked on as Montgomery bent to scoop the bundle of joy into her arms. Back and forth she slightly swayed as she looked down at Emme, who cooed causing Montgomery to smile so brightly that it lit up her face.

That tugged at him.

"I'll leave you alone," the au pair said before exiting the suite.

"Can you believe we're going to have one of our own?" she whispered, looking over at him.

"I can't wait," he admitted.

Patiently, he leaned against the wall and watched her enjoy those precious moments bonding with his niece—*their* niece.

She's my wife. For now anyway.

When Montgomery finally placed the baby in her crib it was with obvious reluctance.

Neither of us thought we wanted a child and now we're anxious for its arrival.

Sean and Montgomery stepped out into the den and the au pair reentered the suite, closing the door behind her. They both paused to see Nicolette exit the elevator with her silver chiffon dress trailing behind her.

He felt Montgomery stiffen beside him and he placed a hand to her lower back.

Nicolette gave them a smile that didn't reach her eyes. "Sean, may I have a moment alone with your wife?" she asked, her hands clasped in front of her.

"No, most definitely not," he said.

Montgomery glanced up at him as he continued to eye his mother. "No more of your covert mission to lay down the law to new members of this family," he said. "Montgomery is pregnant and I will not let you aggravate her with that nonsense, *Maman*."

Nicolette released a gasp of surprise—a momentary lapse before she quickly regained her composure.

"I suggest you take this time to prepare yourself to act appropriately, *Maman*," Sean said. "And when you join the rest of the family be prepared to show happiness when we reveal we have a baby coming."

His mother's blue eyes dropped down to Montgomery's belly. "Congratulations," she said, stepping forward to press a kiss to both of their cheeks. "A baby is always a blessing. Let's go share the good news."

He kept his hand on Montgomery's back, wanting to reassure her as they all stepped onto the elevator and descended back to the first floor. As soon as they stepped into the living room, the entire Cress brood surrounded them with joy.

"Congratulations!" everyone exclaimed.

His mother quietly regained her spot next to Phillip Senior, reaching to take his hand in hers to grasp tightly.

"How did you all know?" Montgomery asked as the women all pressed hands to her belly.

Monica held up the video baby monitor.

They had overheard the news.

As the women whisked her away to start chattering about baby names and clothes, Sean eyed his father, who raised his virgin drink to him in a toast before leaning to whisper something to his wife.

Nicolette rose and crossed the room to leave the living room. She returned after a while with Felice carrying a tray of champagne-filled flutes, which the woman quickly distributed before giving Montgomery a flute with more flavored sparkling water. His mother reclaimed her spot next to his father.

They all looked on as Phillip Senior slowly rose

to his full height from his seat on the sofa—a clear effort on his part.

"As my days feel counted, I am pleased to be able to see and hold another Cress baby," he said with emotions rarely shown by him brimming in his eyes. "I have many regrets, my sons, but never the birth of any of you. Never."

Sean was surprised by their father's impassioned emphasis.

Phillip Senior raised his flute of champagne. "For this, I will drink with you all, my family. *À la nourriture. À la vie. À l'amour,*" he said, resting his eyes on Sean.

To food. To life. To love.

"*À la nourriture. À la vie. À l'amour,*" they all said in unison.

Eight

One week later

Montgomery bit the tip of her stylus as she looked up from her tablet at the light rain drizzling against the windows of Sean's condo. She had been swiping through press clippings of all her firm's clients over the past week. The hour was late and she was home alone.

Sean had left right after their dinner of homemade pizza.

Was she curious where he was and what he was up to? Definitely. Did she ask him for an explanation? Definitely not.

Still, I'm curious.

Had he gone back on his word and was with another woman?

Somehow, she didn't believe that, plus, a lot of the time the press followed his movements so closely that it took a cursory check to discover his activities. Still, it was evidence that Sean Cress was not prepared to settle down. He was a certified bachelor at his core and when their marriage of convenience was over, she was sure he would kick it back into high gear. Women. Parties. Jet-setting.

She had resolved herself to take on the majority of the work of parenting as her ex enjoyed his lavish lifestyle.

And in time, once things were settled and she made a new routine for being a single working mother, she would find her Mr. Perfect—who was interested in being a stepparent. What does that look like? Curious, she opened up her old dating app. She hadn't logged in since she discovered she was pregnant. As she swiped through possible matches, she read the bios of each. Some men unequivocally stated they were not interested in women with children. She paused at the sight of a handsome bearded man with a toothy smile.

"Charles Yaeger. Private school principal. Man of God. Father of one daughter I adore. Looking for a single parent who understands the importance of family, not just dating—although romance is *always* important," she read.

He seemed…perfect.

The lock on the front door disengaged as she closed the app and put to rest any concerns over Charles Yaeger still being available two years later. With a glance back over her shoulder, she eyed Sean entering wearing a tuxedo with his bow tie undone.

He paused at the sight of her as he took off his shoes. "Still up?" he asked.

"Just working and enjoying the view," she said, holding up her tablet.

He walked over to lean against the back of the couch and look down at her with a yawn. "Don't forget I leave tomorrow," he said.

He was doing a new series, highlighting his travels across the continent as he feasted on local cuisine indigenous to the area. He was excited about it and had been preparing by reading up on each country to which he was traveling. It was all he'd talked about for days.

"I didn't," she said. "For a few weeks, right?"

He nodded. "By the time I get back the house should be ready," he said.

"Thanks for overseeing that for me," she told him, tilting her head back on the couch. "And for paying half the bill."

Sean's eyes studied her face. "No problem," he said. "You should turn in, too. Your eyes look tired."

True. He was always so observant.

Montgomery rose, leaving her tablet on the sofa as she followed a yawning Sean across the expansive living space and chef's kitchen to reach the rear where there were four bedrooms.

"'Night, Montgomery," he said as he continued to the master bedroom.

"Sean," she softy called behind him.

He looked over his shoulder.

She beckoned him with her finger. "Three weeks is a long time," she said.

Sean raised both brows as he turned.

Montgomery undid the satin robe she wore and it slid to a puddle at her feet as she turned and leaned in the open doorway with the light of the bedroom outlining her frame.

"Damn," he swore from down the hall.

She smiled.

Moments later his arms were around her and his lips pressed to her neck. She sighed and shivered as she led him into the bedroom. The rustle of fabric let her know he undressed and left a trail of clothing. When they reached the bed, he pressed the length of his hard inches against the groove of her buttocks, naked and warm. He sucked her nape as his hands cupped her breasts and teased her nipples.

No words were needed. Passion spoke.

He kissed her from her shoulders to the back of her knees, pausing to lightly bite each of her soft butt cheeks. And when he rose his hands massaged the length of her back before applying enough pressure to guide her to bend over. She felt him blow a cool stream of air against her pulsing core just before he buried his face to suck her throbbing bud into his mouth from behind.

Montgomery took a deep breath and jerked her head up, causing her hair to fling back from her face. In the round mirror over the dresser, she watched her reflection as she pressed her hands down into the bed and gripped the coverlet as Sean tasted her slowly and with reverence. Her first climax brought tears to her eyes. "Sean!" she cried out in a whimper as she let her head fall back.

He came around her to sit on the bed, gripping her hips to pull her forward to continue his feast as he deeply sucked her taut nipples. With a shudder, her hands gripped his broad shoulders as he brought her to yet another climax.

With her knees already weak and her pulse racing, Sean turned her body and held his inches as he guided her down onto its steel-like hardness. With a lick of her lips, she circled her hips until nearly all of him was inside of her. She felt his thickness. His strength. His heat.

With his face pressed to her back and his arms wrapped around her breasts as he rocked up inside her, Montgomery covered her face with her hands and let her head lay back on his shoulder as he brought her to a third blazing explosion. "Montgomery!" he roughly cried out as he joined her in the rapture.

Sean stood on the balcony of the villa in Rabat, the capital city of Morocco, overlooking the hotel's garden as he sipped a cup of Moroccan coffee brewed with orange blossom water, spices and topped with warm milk. He was enjoying the food and culture of the North African country. With this show, he had a costar who focused more on the sights to see in the beautiful country rich with history. He had taped his conversations with locals as he explored markets and learned more about the spices and local dishes. Tomorrow the chef from the four-star hotel where they stayed was going to walk him through making mint tea, roasted eggplant dip with naan and then a chicken tagine with olive served with seasoned couscous.

It had been a week since he left New York and out-side of the hours they taped, he was feeling bored. Restless.

Alone.

That was surprising.

Sean usually sought solace after long days of film-ing or being socially outgoing. He would enjoy the comfort of his bedroom suite at the townhouse or the quiet of his condo. To think. Read. Sleep.

Now it felt unsettling.

Knock-knock.

With another sip of his drink from the aged bronze cup, Sean crossed the bedroom and opened the door to the hall. It was his cohost, Sara Paul, an Indian beauty with waist-length hair and pert breasts that were currently on display in a sheer nightshirt. She was barefoot, probably sans panties—he couldn't tell—and carrying a bottle of champagne.

Sean eyed her in amusement as he leaned in the doorway, still fully dressed. "And exactly what part of the show is this?" he asked before taking another sip of the brew.

Sara smiled. "Just a little entertaining in the down-time between shoots," she said.

Sean leaned forward to look left and then right down the length of the hall. "People are coming," he advised her.

Sara hid her face with her hands as a middle-aged couple passed by.

"She doesn't have any panties on!" the man whis-pered.

Welp, that answers that, Sean thought.

The stranger glanced back at Sara, earning him a pinch from his wife.

"Sara, I'm here to work not play," he told her, already stepping back and closing the door.

She looked disappointed and pouted. "What happened to the Sean Cress I've heard so much about? The one I saw in the sex tape?" she asked with sultry eyes. "You were…impressive."

"Good night, Sara," he said in a singsong fashion as he closed the door.

"No woman has ever made you weep," she said, pressing her face to the slowly narrowing space between the door and the frame.

Sean closed the door, hoping the woman had stepped back before she was hurt in any way. He had no regrets for turning down her charms.

She was no match to Montgomery.

"I miss your father. I really do," Montgomery said as she looked down at her steadily growing belly.

She knew she shouldn't. It made no sense to get used to him in her life every day when their time being married and living together would end. It was foolish.

But still true.

He called every few days to check on her, but it felt more perfunctory than due to missing her as well.

She attributed her longing for him to craving his sex, but it was more than that. He wasn't there in the morning to fix breakfast or drop her off at work. Attend doctor's appointments. Cook dinner. Make her laugh. Regale with stories from his adventures in celebrity.

Or even to disagree.

On schooling for their child. Private versus public. And the use of nannies. She was against it.

Even how much child support he should pay. The weekly amount he offered was insulting—as if she could not provide a good enough life for their child. Or at least good enough in the eyes of the mighty Cress family.

They were so different.

Still…

Montgomery missed the affable charmer.

Using her thumb, she swiped across her phone to scroll through his social media feed. He was in Greece. Living life to the fullest with a smile bright enough to replace the sun.

"You okay, Go-Go?"

She looked over at her father across the dining room table of his home. They were enjoying dinner together after the Sunday church service. She'd been surprised that he cooked the meal of pot roast and roasted sweet potatoes.

"I'm good. Just wondering when *you* started cooking," she said, being honest.

"Your hubby sent me a care package," he said, using his fork and knife to slice through the tender meat.

"What?" Montgomery exclaimed.

Reverend Morgan shrugged his thin shoulders. "After the storm," he said.

She stood and moved past him to enter the kitchen. It resembled a Cress, INC. showroom. There was a colorful array of pots, bakeware, spices, cookbooks and other accessories. It was an incredibly kind and generous gesture—particularly to a man who openly disapproved and insulted him. She picked up one of the cookbooks to find Sean's smiling face on the cover. She pressed a hand to it.

Sean never said a word.

She returned to her seat in the dining room. "You like the stuff?" she asked.

"It'll do," he said.

Montgomery stiffened. "It'll do?" she repeated with a tinge of annoyance before she could catch herself.

She felt defensive of her husband.

Reverend Morgan picked up the napkin from his lap to wipe both corners of his mouth. She leaned in to see the tag with the Cress, INC. logo on the linen. "My forgiveness is not for sale, Montgomery," he said sternly.

"But it shouldn't be held for emotional ransom, either, Daddy," she muttered before taking a bite of the meat.

"What's that you said?" he asked.

Just then she remembered how Sean had respectfully put his mother in her place and stood up to her foolishness. She admired him for that and wished she had the same courage when it came to her father.

"Nothing, Daddy. Just nothing," she said, focusing on her meal.

Sean dived into the tranquil turquoise waters of the island of Upolu in Samoa, a Polynesian island country. He enjoyed the clear waters and its warmth against his body as he swam what seemed like in-

finite laps before circling back to his thatched-roof
bungalow—one of a dozen on the private beach. As
he left the lagoon and climbed the stairs of the over-
the-water structure, he knew Montgomery would
enjoy such a place.

He paused in drying off with a plush towel at the
thought of her. It seemed a constant—particularly
with each passing day he was away from her.

What's she doing?

Is she being safe?

Is she working too much?

Is she staying calm to get her blood pressure lowered the way the doctor ordered?

They didn't speak as often as he would like because of filming and the time difference. Samoa was
nineteen hours ahead of Eastern Standard Time.

He checked the time on his phone and did the cal-
culations. It was roughly two in the morning in New
Jersey. Although he longed to check in on her, he
didn't have the heart to awaken her. With her full
work schedule and the pregnancy, she needed all the
rest she could get.

Sean did call his brother Lucas.

"Seriously, bro," Lucas said in irritation, his voice
filled with sleep.

"My apologies. I need you to do me a favor," he
said, tucking the phone between his shoulder and ear
as he worked his wet swim trunks down his body to
step out of them.

Nude, he crossed the hexagon-shaped bungalow
to reach the frosted glass bathroom.

"Check on Montgomery for me?" he asked as he turned on the square rain showerhead.

"I can do that," Lucas said.

"What's wrong, baby?" a woman's voice asked.

"It's just my brother," Lucas said to her.

Sean instantly pictured someone buxom and not too bright. It was his brother's type. Of all the brothers, Lucas was the most active with the ladies. Since his weight loss several years ago he was definitely making up for his days being the chubby kid who craved snack cakes more than the attention of girls—just the way their mother liked it. "You home?" he asked.

"Yeah."

"*The* Nicolette Lavoie-Cress is going to flip if she catches another overnight guest in her precious abode," Sean warned, remembering the fit their mother had the last time it happened.

Lucas just laughed.

"The future Mrs. Lucas Cress?" he asked as steam filled the bathroom.

"Definitely *not*," his baby brother stressed.

Sean could only shake his head.

"Did you try the pani popo?" Lucas asked.

Although Lucas was now built tall and lean, the kid who loved sweets was still there. "Yes," he said of the Samoan bread rolls baked in coconut milk sauce. He was the one to tell his acclaimed pastry chef brother about the local delicacy he heard about but hadn't tried until earlier that day during lunch. "Delicious. I damn near ate a pan by myself."

"Great. Now I'm hungry," Lucas said, sounding disgruntled.

"Eat what's in bed with you. No calories," Sean quipped.

Lucas laughed. "I'm in the den so I can talk freely."

"Listen, don't forget about Montgomery," he insisted, returning to the reason for his late-night call.

"Looks like you can't forget about her," Lucas said.

His brother was the only one who knew that his marriage to Montgomery was arranged.

"I do miss her," Sean admitted.

"Maybe the marriage is more real than you want to admit," Lucas offered.

"Noooo," Sean said with a definitive shake of his head. "I like her. We have fun. And she's having my baby—"

"Your *ba-by*," Lucas interjected, obviously still shocked by that.

"Right?" Sean agreed. "But this is not for forever. I need my freedom. This year of marriage is enough for me."

"And Montgomery?"

Sean thought of her. "This whole marriage of convenience was her idea, remember?" he reminded.

"Things change."

Sean shook his head. "But I don't want them to," he insisted. "I've come to grips with fatherhood. I'm ready and eager. Marriage? *Never.*"

"Who are you trying to convince? Me? Or yourself?" Lucas asked. "I know you, big brother, and you've changed for the better since you've been with Montgomery."

"Changed? In what way?"

"Settled. More focused. Less caught up in yourself," Lucas quickly supplied.

Too quickly for Sean, who frowned. "Well, damn. I didn't know I needed changing," he drawled.

"I didn't, either, until I saw the changes."

"It's just me being sure not to embarrass my wife in the press so I'm chilling," Sean said. "But as soon as I'm free I will be living it up again. Watch."

"I hear you."

"But do you believe me?" Sean asked.

"Nope."

Sean chuckled. Lucas was always the most honest with him. Always. "Let me wash my ass and you go enjoy your late-night snack. And strap up," he added. "You see the situation I'm in."

"I got a drawer full."

"'Night, bro."

"'Night."

Sean ended the call and sat the phone on the edge of the semi-recessed sink before opening the glass door and stepping under the spray of water.

Montgomery looked at the pan of rolls then up at Lucas. She took a deep inhale and released a grunt of pleasure. "What are these called?" she asked.

"Pani popo," Lucas said with a smile that reminded her far too much of his older brother.

Lucas Cress, like the other five brothers, was undeniably handsome. He favored former *Bridgerton* actor, Regé-Jean Page, with a shortbread complexion, slashing brows and smoldering eyes.

With a smile, she reached and picked up one of the

sticky rolls from the pan to take a bite. It was light in texture and sweet. Her eyes widened. "That's so good," she sighed with a shimmy of her shoulders.

Lucas moved about the kitchen of the Tribeca condo with ease, gathering saucers, utensils and linen napkins with the comfort of a person who had been there before. "Sean told me about them and I looked up the recipe," he explained where they sat at the island.

"You heard from Sean," she said lightly, trying not to show her disappointment that she had not.

"Yes, at two in the morning," Lucas told her. "He asked me to check on you."

Montgomery smiled.

Lucas chuckled. "He's in Samoa this week and it's nineteen hours ahead," he explained on behalf of his older brother and best friend. "Trust me, you were on his mind."

Montgomery focused on eating more of the roll she held, although her heart wildly pounded.

"How are you feeling?" Lucas asked, his voice serious.

"Good," she told him, picking up her cup of mint tea to sip. "My blood pressure is higher than my doctor likes so I'm working on destressing and cutting back on salt. In fact, I have an appointment tomorrow afternoon."

"Does Sean normally go with you?" Lucas asked.

Montgomery nodded. "Tomorrow is the first he'll miss."

"Then I'll take his place," Lucas declared.

"You don't have to do that," she said, fighting the

temptation for another of the sweet rolls as she kept in mind of gestational diabetes.

They are good, but not that *good.*

"Yes, I do because you're family and we stick together, especially since you are carrying my niece or nephew," he said.

The wealth of the Cress family made her nervous. She worried that their influence and affluence would have a negative effect on her rearing of a child, but one thing she took comfort in was their closeness. She had come to learn that the Cress brothers were close, loving and supportive. Her child would have the best uncles in the world—especially since she wasn't quite sure how involved Sean would be, once they were divorced.

"Okay," she agreed as she pushed the pan of tempting rolls away.

"You done?" Lucas asked with a frown similar to that of his brother.

"If I eat that it will shoot up my blood sugar," she said, using a linen napkin to free her fingers of sticky crumbs.

"And if I eat it, I won't stop and I'll soon be back three sizes bigger," he countered.

They eyed each other and then eyed the rolls.

"Just one won't hurt," Montgomery said.

"And then we'll freeze the rest," Lucas offered, turning to retrieve a box of freezer-safe Ziplocs.

Montgomery eagerly reached to pick up a roll.

Lucas followed suit.

With eyes twinkling with mischief, they touched the pieces of bread together in a toast before devouring them far too quickly.

* * *

It had been three weeks since Sean Cress had been home.

He was exhausted, hungry and slightly out of sorts from the varying time zones across which they traveled to complete the three episodes his producers hoped would lead to a full series order. Sean wasn't so sure of the project anymore. Sara was still far too aggressive in seeking out sex with him, and he spent more time watching other chefs prepare meals than digging in himself.

With a yawn and stretch, he entered his Tribeca condo, letting the leather duffel he carried slip from his shoulder to the floor.

The house was dark and quiet with pockets of lights. In the air was the light scent of Montgomery's perfume. She liked to work in the living room instead of using one of the empty bedrooms during their stay at the condo. Next to the sofa were a pair of the fuzzy slippers she wore around the house. And open on the low-slung living room table was a book on what to expect during pregnancies. He smiled at her laptop on the kitchen island. Next to it, he found a note and a roast beef and provolone sandwich with arugula, sun-dried tomato and red onions on fresh-baked bread.

"Welcome home, Sean. It hasn't been the same without you. Montgomery," he read before looking around the space again.

Somehow the cold and modern bachelor-pad condo felt like home.

He removed the hiking boots he wore with olive

cargo shorts and an orange long-sleeve tee. He went down to the sleeping area and paused at the entry to Montgomery's room. She was in the middle of the bed. He smiled at the sounds of her soft snores. His eyes dipped to the swell of her belly through the covers with her hand resting on it. The urge to undress and climb in the bed just to hold her was strong. And surprising.

I know you, big brother, and you've changed for the better since you've been with Montgomery.

Sean moved away from the doorway and continued down the hall to reach the owner's suite. He undressed, leaving the clothes in a pile by the door, and strode naked to his en suite. He was fatigued but he knew he couldn't properly rest until he washed away the forty-eight hours of filming and then the traveling to get back to America.

"Shower *and* shave," he said, looking at himself in the mirror. His beard was nearly full grown. "Then sandwich and sleep."

With instrumental jazz music playing from a playlist on his phone, Sean made quick work of the beard, using clippers to cut it down to a light shadow. In the shower the feel of the heated water beating against his aching muscles was therapeutic. With a towel draped around his waist, and another quick look at Montgomery asleep in her bed, he made his way to the kitchen to devour the sandwich. It hit the spot.

"Hey."

Over the edge of the glass of milk he poured for himself, Sean eyed Montgomery walking into the kitchen in a pink satin shirtdress and matching fur slippers with her hair up in a ponytail. She looked adorable.

"Hey," he responded, coming around the slate island to pull her in for a hug as he lightly settled his chin atop her head.

Montgomery wrapped her arms around his waist. The baby kicked and they both laughed but continued to hold on to one another.

Fighting his fatigue, Sean swung her body up into his arms. As Montgomery settled her head on his shoulder, he carried her back to her bedroom to lie on her bed. When he stepped back, he felt a draft across his buttocks as she tugged at his towel before dropping it to the floor.

He climbed onto the bed and lay down on his back as he eyed her.

"Tired?" she asked as she climbed onto the bed beside him on her knees.

"Yes," he stressed, easing his hand under her shirt-dress to lightly caress her soft breasts.

Montgomery purred as she sat atop his strong thighs.

Sean gasped when she reached to stroke him. With a moan and a lick of his lips, he worked his hips as she massaged him from root to tip until he was hard. She rose up on her knees and held his dick as she eased down onto him until he filled her.

She was hot and wet and tight. So tight.

Slowly, Montgomery rode him as she pressed her hands down on his chest. He watched her in wonder, amazed at her passion and her stamina. He fed on the pleasure on her face. He reveled in their connection. Their chemistry.

As he felt his release build, Sean reached up to grip the headboard. He felt the muscles of his arms tense. His explosion came and shook him as she continued to ride him through it. It was made all the more intense because she climaxed as well. The clutch of her walls. Her nails digging into his flesh. The pleasure on her face. Her trembles.

"Welcome back," she whispered down to him.

"It's good to be back," he told her in between harsh breaths.

When she tumbled on the bed beside him, Sean turned on his side to gather her body close to his. He pressed a kiss to her nape and settled in to sleep with her in his arms for the rest of the night. He didn't have the energy or the desire to leave her bed.

Nine

"That was delicious, Sean."

Montgomery fought the urge to drag her finger in the drippings left from the salted caramel, pear and walnut Tarte Tatin. Well aware they were in CRESS X in Tribeca, a fine dining establishment, she resisted. Instead, she picked up her margarita mocktail. "Wonderful selections," she said, raising the glass to him in toast of the tasting menu.

He touched his glass to hers before they both took sips and eyed each other over the rims with the hint of flirtation.

In the days since his return, things were different between them.

More lingering touches.

More caresses.

More talking.

More laughing.

More time spent together.

More lovemaking.

It was nice.

Very nice.

Montgomery didn't believe there was anything better than Sean rubbing her entire body down with oil. What started as therapeutic slowly became erotic when his fingers glided over her rounded belly and down in between her thighs to spread them before he stroked her plump mound and teased her pulsing clit.

Memories of her cries of pleasure echoed as she remembered trembling and arching her back off the bed as she gripped the sheets into her fists.

"How is the acquiring of the streaming service coming along?" she asked, purposefully guiding her thoughts away from naughty things with Sean.

He clasped his hands together. "It's a go," he said, his eyes filled with his excitement. "CressTV is happening and will be incorporated under my duties at Cress, INC."

"Congratulations, Sean!" she softly exclaimed.

"There's a lot to figure out with my current contracts to do shows and we're considering whether to delay the launch until those shows have aired or not. Or should we buy out the contract or acquire the rights to the shows," he explained. "There's a lot to consider and to learn. I'm excited."

"And will this secure the CEO position?" she asked just as their server appeared and set glass bowls of beautifully cut and arranged fresh fruit before them.

My favorite.

She selected a grape to pop into her mouth and moaned as she found it to be sweet like cotton candy.

"To be honest, the launch of the streaming service and my current duties will be so time-consuming, that I'm not sure I want the position anymore," he admitted, selecting a star-shaped piece of melon to bite. "As the CEO I would have to appoint a new president to take over my duties supervising the cooking shows. I feel the most excited about CressTV right now."

"And your baby," she reminded him.

Sean smiled. "Of course. I meant work, not personal, Montgomery," he said.

"My mistake," she replied, picking up another grape.

"No worries. You don't make many," he reassured her.

"And some of them turned out for the best," she said, pressing her hands to her belly.

"We're having a baby," Sean said.

"We. Are. Having. A. Baby," she said in mock disbelief.

"A girl with your eyes."

"Or a boy with yours."

They finished their fruit and took their leave, holding hands and talking as they awaited the Bentley at the valet. As they drove home, Sean's phone began to ring. He reached for it. "Yeah."

Montgomery reached into the clutch she carried for her compact to check her makeup and hair.

"We're on the way back from dinner but if you have your key just go in and get it," Sean said.

Just go in and get it?

"Okay," Sean said, finishing the call and setting his phone back on the console.

Montgomery eyed him with curiosity.

"That was Lucas," he supplied. "He needed something out of the condo."

"Something?" she asked, her interest piqued.

"A case of champagne."

"Where?" she asked.

Sean gave her a look as he used one hand to turn the corner. "In the last bedroom," he said.

I never went in the other bedrooms.

"And Lucas has a key?" she asked, thinking of Lucas's familiarity with the home when he came to visit her that day while Sean was in Samoa.

"Yes," Sean said. "Is that a problem?"

Montgomery shook her head. "Of course not. It's not my place. It's yours. I'll be home this week," she said.

Sean reclaimed her hand in his and raised it to press kisses to her fingertips.

But her thoughts were not on seduction.

Champagne in a bedroom?

As they rode up in the elevator, Montgomery leaned back against Sean's chest as he pressed kisses to her temple. "What if we miss each other after the divorce?" he asked, his voice deep and low in her ear.

Montgomery trembled, remembering their first steamy time on an elevator together. "Then we will get over it," she said, turning to look up at him. "Our deal ends with our divorce."

Sean pressed his hands to her face and bent his head to kiss her mouth.

Montgomery gasped in between each one. She

reached up to clutch his elbows as her knees weakened when his kisses shifted down to her throat.

"You sure?" he asked with some of his old bravado.

"Unlike you, Mr. Cress," she said as she leaned back from his heat. "I have every intention of one day finding the man meant for me and walking into marital bliss."

"Mr. Perfect," he said with a hint of sarcasm as he stepped back from her.

"Mr. Perfect for *me*," she stressed, turning as the elevator slid to a stop and the doors opened.

He inclined his head and said nothing, but Montgomery was curious about his thoughts. As they made their way down the hall, their mood had shifted. Their hands were not entwined and the flirtatious warmth with hints of heated passion to come had cooled.

When they entered the already lit condo, Montgomery felt relief to step out of her beloved heels with a sigh. She walked into the kitchen to open the fridge and pull out a bottle of her pear-flavored sparkling water.

Sean settled on the sofa and used the condo's assigned tablet to turn on the television.

The silence was awkward.

Montgomery eyed him, wondering just why his ardor had cooled because she mentioned her intention to remarry. For a second she thought of jealousy but then quickly pushed that aside. Sean's interest in her went only as far as sex and the mothering of his child.

He looked up and caught her eyes on him. He shifted his gaze back to the television screen.

It felt like a rebuke and that stung.

"No late-night parties to attend?" she asked.

He gave her another glance. "If my presence suddenly bothers you, I'm sure I can find something to get into," he said.

"I bet you could," she snapped.

Now he locked his eyes with hers and they were heated. Not with desire but annoyance.

"You probably been finding something else to get into the whole time," she said.

"I'm not the one who pretends to be something I'm not. I don't lie," he shot back.

It landed and emotions pierced her.

"Let me warn you, Sean Cress, I am not the one to verbally spar with," she said, her voice cold.

"Unless I'm your father and then suddenly you'd be *mute*," he said, his voice dripping with sarcasm as he continued to flip through the channels.

That hurt.

"When you're nice, you are very nice, Sean Cress," she said, hating that her voice trembled. "But that was very nasty. And cruel. I guess I was a fool to think you were above that."

She turned and walked away.

"Montgomery," he called behind her.

She ignored him, although she heard his contrite tone.

When she reached the end of the hall leading to the bedrooms, she looked to the right at the door she had never opened in the past month. She closed the distance and wrenched the knob before pushing it open.

"What?" she exclaimed, seeing the cases upon cases of liquor that lined the walls.

She stopped counting at more than two dozen different brands. She turned to see him standing in the hall with his hands dug into the pockets of his tailored black slacks. "Sean," she said with concern. "Was this your party pad?"

"I've had parties here, yes," he admitted.

"So much so that you keep inventory for a liquor store on hand?" she asked, unable to hide her astonishment.

Sean chuckled. "I'm a grown man, this is my home and this is not Prohibition, Montgomery," he said.

She looked back at the abundance of alcohol and then at him. "You gave me the impression that you barely stayed here. Like it was an investment property," she said.

"Both are true."

She frowned.

"Why are you spoiling for a fight?" he asked before stepping back to lean his tall frame against the wall as he continued to watch her.

"I don't want to fight," she said.

"What do you want, Montgomery?" he asked.

"To know if you ever had women here?" she asked.

He shifted his eyes away.

Montgomery winced. "Sean," she said, awaiting an answer.

He looked back at her. "Yes," he admitted.

"Flings?" she asked as her heart pounded and she felt anger she couldn't explain.

No, he wasn't her husband at the time.

No, their marriage wasn't meant to last.

No, he owed her no explanation.

Still...

She eyed him, not hiding the hurt she felt even if she couldn't fully grasp the reason for it.

His silence was telling.

With a nod, she licked her lips. "Feels great to be one of the number of women you screw here," she said, her voice low and numb as she leaned in to close the door and then came down the hall.

He stepped in her path. "I never looked at you that way, Montgomery," he said with earnest.

"The idea of living here now feels the same as me visiting the Playboy mansion," she said with a shrug of her shoulders. "It's a no for me."

He reached for her and she shirked away from his touch before continuing down the hall to enter her room and close the door behind her.

Knock-knock.

"Montgomery, let's talk about this," he said through the wood of the door.

She locked it and moved to lie across the foot of the bed. When she heard his footsteps echo as he moved away from the door, she felt relief. As she lay in the darkness and clutched one of the throw pillows on the bed to her chest, Montgomery wrangled with her emotions.

Foremost was her confusion.

She was well aware of Sean's past—she served as his publicist/crisis manager for the release of a sex tape—but still, it bothered her. It burned in her gut. It kept her from getting a restful night of sleep. Anytime she closed her eyes, visions of Sean and a bevy of women enjoying a late night of lascivious partying in the condo plagued her.

And she hated it.

She wasn't quite sure why in her visions Sean was wearing chaps sans pants and standing atop a table as he poured magnums of champagne upon the exposed breasts of the women looking up at him in adoration.

"Go, Sean! Go, Sean! Go, Sean!" the women chanted in her visions.

I have a headache.

She was thankful for sleep although it was restless. Her thoughts remained troubled even at work the next day.

With a sigh, Montgomery entered her office and closed the door, momentarily leaning against it before she continued across the space to her desk. Hanna had ordered lunch but she ignored hers as she reached for her phone to pull up the contact information for the electrician working on her house.

As the phone rang, she picked up the clear plastic container of grilled chicken atop arugula salad only to sit it back down before tapping the tips of her nails against the desk.

"Hello," Ernesto said loudly with the sound of drilling in the background.

"Hi. This is Montgomery. I know you've been in contact with my husband, Sean Cress—"

"Yes! Great guy," Ernesto said.

Montgomery held back on making a snide comment on just how friendly that great guy was. "I was just wondering when the electrical work would be done," she said.

"We wrapped up two weeks ago, Mrs. Cress," Ernesto said. "Hold on. One sec."

She tensed.

Ernesto gave orders to his crew.

Two weeks ago?

"Mrs. Cress, we have an emergency here, but I assure you the job is complete. My bill was paid in full and I hope you both will call on me again if you need further electrical work," he rushed to say.

"But I have questions," she insisted.

"Okay. Can I call you back? Please," he stressed.

"Yes," she said.

He ended the call.

This makes no sense.

She started to call Sean but decided against it because he had lied to her about the status of the house. "Why?" she asked herself aloud.

One thing was true about Sean Cress. He was no liar. At times he was too honest.

Or was he too good to be caught?

Montgomery quickly gathered her keys, her bag and her briefcase before she strode out of her office. Hanna paused in taking a bite of her own salad. "Finish your lunch. I have to make a run and I'll be back in an hour. If that changes, I'll call and update you," she said, quickly moving past the young woman's desk.

"Is everything okay?" Hanna called behind her, drawing the curious stares of Montgomery's other employees.

She glanced back over her shoulder. "I hope so," she said, pushing the front door to leave the offices on the fifth floor of the thirty-story building.

Even last night as they argued he could have told her the electrical repairs were complete.

Did something go wrong?

Did he have to hire someone to come behind Ernesto?

Once in her car, Montgomery made good time getting from Manhattan to Passion Grove. As she drove up the drive, it felt good to see her home again—and it would even be better to be back in it again.

She unlocked the front door and stepped inside but paused. "Oh my," she sighed.

The smell of paint was strong and absolutely nothing about the house looked recognizable. She felt like she was on a home makeover show and it was time for the big reveal. With her mouth open, she moved about the entire home, amazed at all of the renovations and upgrades. She gently touched it all. Walls removed. New floors and paint. Updated fireplaces. Reconfigured kitchen. Her bedroom was now made into an owner's suite with its own attached bathroom. Even the basement was now finished and fully decorated as a theater room with its own bathroom and pantry.

It had to be the work of Sean.

"Oh, Sean," she sighed, pressing her hands to her cheeks and finding them flushed with heat.

Over their months together she had briefly mentioned plans she had for her 1940s home but never had she guessed he would take those ideas and make them a reality. With the same attentiveness he gave to remembering her love of fruit on their airplane ride or being sure her favorite drink was stocked at his parents'—she never even knew he was paying such close attention.

And then truth settled in. The reason she was so annoyed by the thought of him with other women. Why she missed him so much. Why their lovemaking shook her to her very core. Why his smile brought her so much joy.

Tears welled and she didn't contain them. They wet her fingers.

I love him.

But her heart was broken.

As much as she longed for love in her life, never did she want it to be unrequited.

And the man made it so very hard *not* to love him.

To want him.

To have him.

Montgomery sank on her sofa, wishing he was everything she envisioned for herself. Her Mr. Perfect. The love of her life.

But he wasn't and he didn't want to be.

What am I going to do?

Sean drove up the drive of Montgomery's house and parked behind her vehicle before exiting and making his way to the front door. It opened and there she stood.

Her eyes were red and puffy. Her arms were crossed over her chest as if consoling herself.

That tore at him.

"How can I thank you for the house?" she asked, her voice soft. "It's beautiful. It's perfect."

A tear raced down her cheek before she lowered her head.

"Montgomery, what's wrong?" he asked, stepping closer to wrap her in his arms.

For a moment, as he massaged her back, she leaned her head against his chest.

"You're killing me. Tell me what's wrong," he said, pressing kisses to her temple as he held her tighter. "How can I fix it if I don't know what's wrong?"

She stepped back out of his embrace and wiped her tears with the sides of her hands. "You can't fix it," she said, running one hand through her hair as she looked over at him.

Sean slid his hands into the pockets of the slacks of his tailored suit. It was to keep from reaching for her.

"I love you," Montgomery admitted before another round of tears. "And that was not a part of the plan."

He was stunned. His heart pounded. Hard and fast. He freed his hands to use one to wipe his mouth as he eyed her and saw in the depths of her eyes her feelings for him.

But he didn't know what to say.

He didn't know what she wanted him to say.

All he knew was she was hurting and that pained him.

"Montgomery," he said, taking a step toward her.

She held up a hand to stop him. "I'm in too deep and I gotta get out," she said, beginning to slowly pace in the area between the living and dining areas. "The sex. The closeness. My jealousy over your past. All of your nice thoughtful gestures. I need space. I need to get over this because we have to raise a child together."

He watched solemnly as she pressed her hands to her rounded belly and let her head fall back with her eyes closed as more tears fell.

"Montgomery, please," he begged, taking steps toward her.

Needing to hold her.

With a shake of her head, she denied him before releasing a shaky breath that seemed to reverberate.

"I'll repay you for this," she said, looking around at the house.

"No," he said sternly. "I did this for you and the baby. I never expected you to repay me. I never even cashed the check you gave me for the electrical work."

"Of course you didn't," she said.

That made him smile a little.

"It's perfect. It's everything I wanted for my home and more," she said, walking over to grip the back of one of the new tufted dining room chairs before she looked back at him over her shoulder. "How can I not love you?"

His chest tightened.

"But I gotta get over it. I have to get over you," she said, trying to sound practical as she looked away from him.

Sean looked around at the house, curious what brought her back to it early. The final work to be completed before he wanted to surprise her was painting the exterior. For weeks the excitement of surprising her had him delirious with anticipation. Over and over he would imagine the look on her face. He had been distracted with pleasing her.

"New plan," she said, clasping her hands together. "We live separately but make appearances together to keep up the ruse."

No.

"Whatever you need, Montgomery," he said, walking over to lightly grip the back of her head as he pressed a kiss to her cheek.

She looked up at him.

They locked eyes.

That undercurrent of awareness and desire that constantly throbbed between them was just as present as ever.

It was tempting.

God, she's beautiful.

The *very* last thing Sean wanted to do at that moment was release her and leave.

But he did.

He *had* to.

Two weeks later

Sean stared down into the brown depths of his drink as he leaned against the wall of the superyacht. When a vision of Montgomery appeared instead, he swirled the alcohol to make it disappear, sending some of the brandy over the side of the snifter.

But I gotta get over it. I have to get over you, Montgomery had said.

"Shit," he swore, gripping the glass.

With a breath he looked around at the celebrity-filled party. Loud music. Gyrating bodies on the dance floor. The loud chatter of talking voices. Flashing lights.

In the past he would have been making his rounds, talking to celebrity friends, posing for pictures and having one hell of a good time. Now that seemed impossible for him.

I love you, Sean.

During the past two weeks, he had tried everything he could to forget the last time he saw Montgomery. Parties during the Cannes Film Festival on the French Riviera. Movie premieres. Club openings. All the while fending off questions about the whereabouts of his new bride.

What he'd learned was his taste for the fast-paced celebrity life was over.

The music too loud.

The conversations too trite.

The hour too late.

I know you, big brother, and you've changed for the better since you've been with Montgomery.

With a scowl, Sean finished the drink in one gulp before making his way through the crowd to the bar to have another.

How can I not love you?

She haunted him.

He missed her and in his own way, he had to get over her, too.

Her smile.

The scent of her perfume.

The sound of her laugh.

The sweetness of her kiss.

Even her soft snores.

And once he returned from traveling, they had slept together. Holding her and having her near while he slept gave him the best rest. He hadn't had another since she returned to Passion Grove. Tossing and turning had become his nightly ritual.

With another curse Sean finished his drink and

made his way off the yacht. He was thankful for Colin as he felt the effects of the alcohol.

"Home?" Colin asked from the driver's seat. "Or another location, sir?"

"Tribeca," Sean said, leaning his head against the rest. "Thanks, Colin."

"Everything okay?" the driver asked.

Sean stared out the window of the moving vehicle. "No," he said, sounding as disgruntled as he felt.

The men rode in silence until Colin pulled to a stop outside Sean's Tribeca apartment building. With effort, Sean left the rear of the vehicle.

"Flowers and a nice night out together usually get me out of the dog house with the missus," Colin offered.

Sean just gave him a smile of thanks and closed the door. The night doorman of the postwar building held the door for him. As he crossed the lobby, he checked the time on his phone. It was nearly two in the morning.

When Montgomery lived with him and he had a late night out, she would be waiting up for him—pretending to work or to read, but up. Like she made sure he got home safely.

As he unlocked the front door of his apartment and entered, his eyes went to the empty sofa. Gone was any sign that Montgomery had once lived there. Now the silence he once sought felt mocking.

I need to get over her, too.

That was turning out to be easier said than done.

"Come back to bed."

Sean frowned at the woman's voice that echoed from down the hall.

Montgomery?

With his heart seeming to slam against his chest from the rush of surprise and happiness, Sean took long but quick strides down the hall to Montgomery's old bedroom.

He frowned at the woman sitting in the middle of the bed, her nudity evident under the sheet clinging to her frame. "Who the hell are you?" he barked.

The woman shrieked. "Oh, my God. It's Sean Cress," she said, clapping her hands together and causing the sheet to fall to her waist.

Sean turned his back to her before he caught sight of her breasts.

"My bad, bro."

Lucas.

"Is your *date* covered?" he asked.

"I don't have to be," the woman said in a girly-like voice that would shred his nerves.

Sean worked his shoulders. "Let me say I now see how *Maman* feels, Lucas," he said, hearing his own annoyance.

"See. You changed," Lucas said in an "I told you so" tone.

"Sean, can I have an autograph?" the woman asked with a giggle.

"Kimmie, my brother is *not* signing your breasts," Lucas drawled.

"Why?" she wailed.

With a shake of his head, Sean left the room. He'd taken a few steps but backtracked to lean in backward to pull the door closed on their shenanigans.

Ten

One week later

Montgomery sat in the middle of the bed with her feet propped up on pillows. Per her doctor's orders, she was on bed rest due to the risk of preeclampsia. She looked at her swollen ankles and feet that had her in flat shoes. It felt odd walking in them, but she had no choice because her beloved heels were no longer comfortable or practical.

"You owe me," she said, looking down at her belly that nearly blocked any view of her upper thighs.

She looked to her open front door at the sound of noises echoing from the kitchen. She knew her father was in her new kitchen, wearing his Cress,

INC. apron and cooking something from one of his cookbooks.

Montgomery sighed.

When he called to reprimand her and Sean for missing church, Montgomery told him Sean was traveling for work and her activities had been limited by her doctor. Her father had made it his duty to stay with her until Sean's return—which only she knew was never going to happen.

She was tired of half-truths.

Lies.

To her father.

To herself.

To the world.

To Sean.

Although their new agreement was to put up a front for their families, Montgomery was nowhere near ready to be under the same roof with Sean again. Her love for him was still strong—maybe even stronger from missing him so much. And so when he called her to ask if he could still attend doctor's appointments with her, Montgomery had begged off. Then he called afterward to see how it went and she told him everything was going well.

Yet another lie.

She shifted to find comfort in the bed and then leaned back against the plush pillows stacked behind her. She felt weepy and took a deep breath hoping to defeat her poignant sadness. All of her plans and she'd left her heart unprotected. Not once had she factored love into the equation.

The best laid plans of mice and men often go awry.

She softly smiled as she remembered Sean's words.

"I still can't believe how good this house looks," Reverend Morgan said, walking in carrying a tray. "Your grandparents would be proud. It's a showcase."

"Sean did it all," she reminded him for what seemed the dozenth time.

"He's all right," her father said begrudgingly, setting the tray on the bed beside her.

He's more than all right.

She looked down at the bowl of grilled chicken fettuccine Alfredo with a side of steamed broccoli. "That looks good, Daddy, but I'm not hungry," she said. "I feel a little nauseated and my back hurts."

"Anything I can get you?" he asked, moving the tray to sit on the bedside table.

She shook her head as she smoothed her hands over her belly.

Her father frowned. Deeply. "Your husband should be here with you," he said. "Not gallivanting over the world. What kind of father will *he* be?"

One who lets his child be who he or she wants to be. Who takes care of his child the way he takes care of strangers. And loving, like he is with his family.

"Daddy, I'm going to take a nap," she said, shifting down on the bed.

"What type of future will the two of you have if he's not here when you need him?" Reverend Morgan continued, his voice rising.

Montgomery closed her eyes. "Daddy, please," she stressed, feigning a yawn and hoping he took the hint.

"This is what happens when you rush into a marriage with someone you don't know," he continued.

"Daddy—"

"This house is beautiful but it's a thing. A possession. What you need more than his money is his presence! And he has the *audacity* to tell me I'm holding you emotionally hostage," her father said, his deep voice dripping with sarcasm. "And about expecting perfection."

Montgomery sat up again—with effort. "What did he say about perfection?" she asked.

Reverend Morgan looked confused. "What?"

"What did Sean say about perfection?" she repeated.

Her father frowned. "Something about all men making mistakes and that no one is perfect or should *expect perfection*," he said, mimicking Sean and using his hands to do air quotes.

No one is perfect.

Like I tried to pretend to be for my father.

Or should expect perfection.

Like I expected from Sean—or any other man to be a part of my life.

The weight of the irony—and her hypocrisy—settled in.

"Emotional blackmail," her father snarked.

Montgomery, a part of your father seeing you as more than his little girl is you presenting yourself as more than that, Sean had said.

"It was," Montgomery said softly, her eyes downcast on her belly and not on her father.

"What?" he asked.

"You cut me out of your life because you didn't approve of a decision I made for *my* life," she said, her tone strengthening as she raised her eyes and locked them with her father's. "That hurt…and it made me so angry with you."

Reverend Morgan scowled. "Angry?" he asked, appearing astonished by her revelation. "Did I dishonor you?"

"No. I dishonored myself by pretending to be perfect to make you happy," she said. "I got good grades. I never talked back. I agreed to your every wish—like giving up swimming even though I used to love it. I made sure to never rock the boat and displease you."

"I never asked you to be perfect, Go-Go," he said, sinking down to sit on the foot of the bed.

"No, but you implied if I didn't you would judge me," she said. "And the one time I made a mistake that you *know* about you did even more than judge. You amputated me from your life for weeks."

She was surprised he showed regret at his actions.

"I was hurt and angry with you," he explained.

"I have never completely felt like myself around you because I never let you know who I am—which is *far* from perfect," she said.

His stare became accusing.

"Dad, my desire to have your approval was so strong that when I got pregnant by Sean, I asked him to marry me for a year so that I wouldn't have to admit the truth," she told him, even as her stomach seemed to flip-flop.

Reverend Morgan jumped to his feet and stepped back from her as if repelled.

"So what now, Dad? Are you going to block me

out of your life again?" she asked, her eyes filling with tears. "Your grandchild, too?"

His eyes went down to her belly and then up to her face again.

"I never wanted to be anything less than perfect for you," she continued. "And without even knowing I sought that same perfection in others. I was wrong on both accounts."

Perfection in any one person doesn't exist.

"I became what I..." She let the words trail.

"That you what?" he asked.

"I became what I resented," she finished.

His face contorted with pain. "You resent me?" he asked, his deep voice a harsh whisper.

"Although you preach about forgiveness and grace, you offered me none," Montgomery countered.

Reverend Morgan picked up the tray and turned to leave the room, the slope of his shoulders dejected.

"Dad, I love you and some of this dynamic between us is my fault for not ever being honest with you," she said, feeling pain for causing him any. "I forgive you and I want us to have a better relationship. A real one with flaws and all. I hope you want the same and can forgive me, too."

He paused in the open doorway and gave her a brief look back before he left the room and closed the door.

The Cress brothers as a collective drew nearly every eye of the women—single and taken—at CRESS IX in Washington, D.C. Sean paid the attention no heed as he reached forward to refill his wineglass. Once they decided to catch up with each other over dinner and drinks, they agreed to do a pop-in of one of the family restaurants and hopped on the jet. He was thankful for the company of his brothers as he fought to deal with not seeing Montgomery. Her need for distance was so great that she hadn't wanted him at the most recent prenatal appointment.

That had hurt him.

He had come to enjoy seeing the growth of their baby and learning of its milestones while sharing in that with her.

And how much time would she need? Will I be able to see my child?

"What's going on with you, Sean? You're not your normal charming and happy self."

He eyed Coleman as he tipped his head back to drain the goblet of the wine he just poured.

"I'm fine," Sean said, turning in his seat to motion with his fingers for their server.

He didn't miss that his five brothers shared looks as he ordered a round of drinks—harder than the award-winning wine they had been enjoying.

"I've never seen you miss a chance to flirt with a woman and you've ignored about a dozen since we arrived," Phillip Junior supplied as he reached for handmade chocolate they had for dessert.

Flirtations?

He hadn't flirted, dated or sexed another woman since Montgomery and had no desire to.

"Not even photos or autographs with his fans," Gabriel added.

Sean ignored them, thankful when the server returned with a tray of six drinks.

"Talk about it. Maybe we can help," Lincoln offered.

Sean said nothing and the normal ambiance of the restaurant echoed.

"He misses his wife," Lucas supplied, drawing a hard look from Sean. "And is miserable because of it. Trust me, we all miss the life of the party."

The brothers toasted to that, causing Sean to deeply frown. "Jerks," he muttered.

But they weren't. These were his brothers. Four he grew up with and one he had grown to love just as much as the rest. Some older. Most were younger. None meant him any harm.

"Marriage is not for me," he said.

"Is it marriage or Montgomery?" Lincoln asked.

"Marriage," Sean asserted without hesitation.

If he ever had the inclination to share the rest of his life with someone it would be Montgomery.

"To hell with being alone," Coleman said. "For me, there is nothing better than sharing my life with Jillian."

"Damn right," the other married brothers agreed.

"After all the years we've been together, Raquel and I have our own language," Phillip Junior told him. "What would take fifty words to explain to everyone sometimes just takes a look with my wife."

Gabriel took a sip of his brandy. "There's nothing better than climbing into bed next to Monica—especially now with Emme lying there between us," he said. "For me, it's the best part of my day."

Sean thought of doing just that with Montgomery and their child.

"I like my freedom," Sean said, more to himself than them.

"*Listen,*" Lincoln said, drawing the eyes of all his younger brothers. "Give up whatever burden you believe marriage to be and get rid of your fear about losing your independence. Realize life can be just as good with someone as you *think* it is without someone."

His brothers all agreed—even single Lucas.

Sean fell silent as he sipped from his drink. There was only one thing he knew for sure. When he had the Passion Grove house remodeled for Montgomery—paying whatever cost to ensure it was done efficiently and quickly—he had envisioned living there *with her.*

Bzzzzzzzzz. Bzzzzzzzzz. Bzzzzzzzzz.

All of the men reached for their phones to see if it was theirs that vibrated.

Sean frowned at the unfamiliar New Jersey number. "Hello," he said after answering.

"Sean? Sean, this is Montgomery's father. Reverend Morgan," the man said, his voice trembling.

He sat up straight. "What's wrong?" he asked.

Five pairs of eyes settled on him.

"It's Montgomery. She went into labor early. We're headed to the hospital. She wants you there," he said. "No. She says to tell you she *needs* you there."

I love you, Sean.

"I'm on the way. Which hospital?" he asked, already rising to his feet.

Fear and panic nearly weakened him. She was over a month early.

Father God, please look out for Montgomery and our child.

Sean strode through the restaurant at full speed, but it still didn't stop the hard pounding of his heart.

"Sean!"

He stopped and turned. His brothers stood standing around the table staring at him in bewilderment. He'd forgotten them. He reached for his wallet as he made his way back to them. He threw a wad of hundred-dollar bills on the table. "We have to get to New Jersey. Montgomery's in labor," he said.

"Already?" Gabriel asked.

Sean nodded and hid not one bit of his fear from his eyes. "It's early," he said.

Lincoln signaled for the server and handed him all of the cash.

The Cress brothers walked out together and quickly made their way to the three-row chauffeur-driven SUV awaiting them. Sean said nothing as they climbed in. He sat on the middle seat between Lucas and Lincoln. As Lucas urged the driver to get back to the airport as quickly as possible, Lincoln called the pilot to re-route their flight to New Jersey instead of New York and the other brothers all called their wives to tell the news, Sean clutched his hands together tightly in the space between his knees to keep them from visibly trembling. He was acutely aware he was not just surrounded by his brothers, but also supported by them. He was grateful. Without them, as his fears and concern about Montgomery and their baby consumed him, he knew he would have felt more alone than ever before in his life.

During the entire trip back, the mood was solemn.

Sean tore through the hospital, leaving his brothers behind, to reach the maternity ward. Reverend Morgan sat in the waiting room wringing his hat in his hands. He stopped with his chest heaving. "How are they?" he asked in between pants.

The man rose to his feet, his face despondent and his eyes brimming with tears. "It's M-M-Montgomery," he stammered. "They don't know if she's going to make it."

Sean shook his head, denying the words. And then he thought of a world without Montgomery in it.

I love you, Sean.

He could picture her so clearly wearing her heart on her sleeve and proclaiming her love for him with no shame.

Will that be the last time I saw her alive?

"No. No," Sean whimpered as he dropped to his knees and covered his face with his hands, feeling completely shattered.

Somewhere in the midst of his grief, he felt strong hands lift him to his feet.

"Sit him here," one of his brothers said.

Lincoln.

"We're here, bro," another said.

Lucas.

Sean looked up at his baby brother, his best friend, as his eyes burned with his tears. "She might not make it," he said.

"Have hope," Lucas said, pushing napkins into his hand. "Don't give up."

I love you, Sean.

"I need her in my life," Sean said, unable to deny his feelings any longer and regretting that he hadn't admitted that to her or himself. "And the baby."

"Trust me," Lucas said, taking the unused napkins to brush the tears from his brother's face. "We all know you do."

Two weeks later

With tenderness, Sean stroked Montgomery's cheek as he looked down at her face. She appeared peacefully sleeping, but all of the medical equipment being used on her was evidence she was in a medically induced coma to give her time to heal from the seizures and stroke brought on by eclampsia. As he worshipped her with his eyes, the sound of "Dream a Little Dream of Me" by Ella Fitzgerald and Louis Armstrong played from his phone. Every day he came to the hospital, sat at her bedside, talked to her and played that song while he was there.

"While I'm alone and blue as can be, dream a little dream of me," he whispered into her ear along with the song.

He could only hope that she did just that as she rested.

Sean pressed kisses to her face as his heart swelled with emotions he could no longer deny. Not anymore. "Come back to me, Montgomery," he begged of her.

He longed for the day she looked up at him with those most beautiful eyes and said the words he needed to hear.

I love you, Sean.

With his hands pressed to her cheeks, he pressed his mouth to the side of hers and let his forehead lightly rest atop hers before he reclaimed his seat beside the bed. He gathered one of her hands between both of his and listened to the jazz classic as he willed her to awaken and return to him.

To us.

Their son was born premature but healthy. Morgan Sean Cress. Just the way Montgomery wanted it.

"He's beautiful," he told her with a smile. "You got your boy with my eyes. And my dimples. But he has your chin."

He eyed her and ached that she had never seen or held their son.

"Dream a little dream of me," Ella Fitzgerald sang.

He winced and looked away from her. At times, seeing her in that way felt like pure torture.

"How is she?"

Sean looked to the door to find Reverend Morgan walking in, hat in hand. "The same," he said. "But the doctor said there's been improvement of her vitals. She's hopeful."

"Then we'll be hopeful," his father-in-law said.

Sean nodded as he rose to his feet and stood by the bed to look down at his wife. His everything.

I know that now more than ever.

"It's high past time I thanked you."

Sean looked across the bed at the older man. "For?"

"Take your pick. The gift from your family's company. The talks even when I didn't want to listen. For loving my daughter. My grandson," he said before clearing his throat. "She told me the truth about the baby and the marriage."

Sean looked down at Montgomery, feeling proud of her.

"I just want my daughter back," the reverend said. "I have so many regrets. I want things to be different between us."

Sean gave him a smile that still had a hint of his sadness. "Same," he agreed. "If she'll let me."

"Same," her father agreed before bending to press a kiss to her forehead.

Soon, Sean took his leave with one last look back at her. As they did every day, the men took shifts sitting at her bedside. Sean would go home and then make hourly calls to the nurses' station for updates on Montgomery's condition. Outside of handling the business side of Montgomery Morgan Publicity while her staff stepped in to cover her PR duties, that was his life for the past two weeks. Everything else had come to a halt. No filming. No meetings. No work.

Things had changed. *He* had changed. For the better.

Sean drove to the Passion Grove house, but when he unlocked the door to enter, he felt the way he always did without Montgomery being there. It was just a house and not a home.

Bobbie and Lincoln looked up at him from where they sat on the sofa together.

"Thanks," Sean said, dropping his keys on the metal table in the foyer and using the large bottle of sanitizer on his hands before moving over to the smart bassinet to look down at his son swaddled and sleeping away. "How was he?"

"Perfect," Bobbie said, pushing her wild curls back from her face before leaning forward to look down at Morgan as well. "There is nothing better than the smell of a baby."

Lincoln eyed his wife with love and indulgence.

In the past week since Sean had brought the baby home, his family rotated sitting with the baby while he visited Montgomery in the hospital, but he took care of Morgan by himself. The nurses at the hospital had prepared him for caring for the baby before he was released to him. With every passing day his nervousness of his son's small size faded. His hands shook a little less as he fed him by bottle, bathed him, changed his diapers and swaddled him. All while talking to him softly about his mother.

"You sure you don't want a nap before we go?" Lincoln asked.

Sean shook his head as he bent to scoop the baby up into his arms. "Morgan and I need to have a man-to-man talk about his mom doing much better today," he said, raising the bundle to press kisses to his brow.

"I made you a seafood lasagna," Lincoln informed him as he followed Bobbie to the front door.

"I appreciate that," Sean said, meaning it.

The help of his parents, his brothers and his sisters-in-law touched him deeply. He wasn't sure how he would ever repay them except to be there in the same way if they ever needed him.

Once they left, he locked the door behind them and warmed one of Morgan's bottles before carrying the baby upstairs to his nursery decorated in shades of cream and deep blue. He settled on one of the matching gliders of navy with cream trim, propping one leg up on the matching ottoman as he gently swayed back and forth.

Morgan opened his eyes and smiled, revealing his dimples. Although he knew his son could only see blurry images, he still smiled down at him as love warmed his entire body. "Hey, little man. You hungry?" he said, introducing the nipple into the baby's mouth the way the nurses taught him. Soon, the gentle sounds of his sucking could be heard. "How are you? You miss me? Because I missed you. Guess who else misses you? Your momma. And I know she's just as ready to wake up and see you as you are to see her."

Sean fed his son, careful to burp him in between, and then changed his diaper not long after. As he rocked him back to sleep, he eased his pinky against Morgan's palm and softly hummed "Dream a Little Dream of Me."

Eleven

One week later

It was a standoff.

As Sean sat across from his parents, Nicolette and Phillip Senior, his eyes fell to his son being held by his mother. He fought an urge to take Morgan from her arms.

"What part of living your own lives is this?" Sean drawled.

Nicolette and Phillip Senior shared a look. "Sean, what if Montgomery doesn't…recover?" she said, casting her solemn gaze on him as she slowly shifted her knees back and forth to rock Morgan in her lap. "You can't continue to raise him alone like this, son. Come home."

The thought of losing Montgomery forever was his constant fear and it tore at his gut like claws. He also worried if he would be able to do it alone, but he couldn't deny that he knew Montgomery's issue. "No," he said with finality. "Montgomery did not want our child raised like *that*—the wealth."

Nicolette looked disbelieving. "Who would deny a child such privilege?" she asked.

"One afraid that it may shape him to be entitled, my love," Phillip Senior said. "It's the same reason I made the fight for CEO so hard for our sons. I wanted them to work for it and not feel entitled to it—especially Phillip Junior."

That surprised Sean. It was a revelation he hadn't anticipated. The missing link to the puzzle of why the same parents who raised them to be close-knit, loving and loyal, had then pitted the brothers against each other to claim the prize of CEO. And in the beginning, the race to the finish had put a strain on their closeness—something they were still working to repair.

Sean looked into the unlit fireplace, squinting as he fit all of the puzzle pieces together. He shifted his gaze to his father, who was smiling down at his grandson. "Phillip Junior will be appointed CEO," he said.

Nicolette and Phillip Senior shared another of their furtive glances—they'd shared many over their decades together—but neither confirmed nor denied his theory.

Sean thought of his own ambivalence over the CEO position. That plus his concerns about Montgomery's recovery made whether or not Phillip Junior had been victorious in securing the position of little importance to him.

Nothing mattered but bringing Montgomery home to our son.

"Please think about our offer, Sean," Nicolette said, raising the baby to snuggle her nose against his cheek. "Let your family help you."

Sean stood up and gave them a forced smile as he crossed the room to press a kiss to the top of his mother's head. "Thank you for helping me by watching your grandson while I go visit his mother," he said, eyeing his sleeping son with adoration. "That is all the help I need."

"But Sean—"

His father's hand to his wife's arm stopped her words.

"Let him be, my love," Phillip Senior said.

Sean raised his chin toward the baby station he set up in the living room for them. "There's bottles, diapers, wipes, a few extra outfits—"

Nicolette laughed. "I raised five sons and nothing in childcare has changed since then," she said.

Sean chuckled. "Right. Okay," he said. "And don't call in a nanny or au pair. Montgomery wouldn't want that. If he gets to be too much or you have something to do, I have Jillian on standby."

His mother looked slightly offended but thankfully said nothing.

After ensuring Montgomery's bedroom and office were locked to prevent his mother from snooping, Sean left them to be driven to the nearby hospital by Colin. His hand gripped Morgan's empty car seat. Missing him already and wondering how he could have ever thought fatherhood would be a burden to his life. For the past few weeks, his life revolved around his son and he couldn't imagine it being any different anymore.

But it can.

When—not if—Montgomery awakened he was aware she may not want him around as much. He could be relegated to a part-time father. A visitor in his son's life. She may still want time to get over him and meet her Mr. Perfect one day. She may not forgive him for not returning the love she professed.

All he knew was he enjoyed waking up every morning and standing over Morgan's crib as his son awakened at the same time each day.

All of that could go away.

Still, to have Montgomery back beautiful and lively as ever in her beloved heels and brightly colored wardrobe was the greatest desire.

I want her back.

He picked up his phone and pulled up the email from the Vegas photographer with all of their digital photos from the wedding. He swiped through them, ending with the one they used on the cover of *Celebrity Weekly*. It was the moment he didn't go for the kiss. The one he had regretted—and still did. She looked so beautiful that night.

It was a huge contrast from the woman constricted by medical equipment.

He set the phone down on the seat beside him.

"Everything okay?" Colin asked.

He forced a smile as he looked at his driver eyeing

him in the rearview mirror. "Just thinking of my wife," he admitted, his sadness feeling like a second skin.

"You two came a long way from that first car ride," Colin said. "And you've got even further to go."

I hope.

"Thanks, Colin."

At the hospital, as the sounds of New Jersey in the summer echoed loudly around him, he exited the vehicle and accidentally knocked his phone from the seat and down onto the concrete pavement. "Damn it," he swore, bending to pick up the device. The screen was shattered.

"Great," he muttered, sliding it into the back pocket of his denims before entering the hospital already.

As he did every day, Sean stopped at the gift shop and purchased a fresh bouquet of flowers before he would make his way up to the intensive care unit. "May I use your phone?" he asked the sales clerk, who looked at him with flirty eyes that he ignored.

"Of course," she said.

With a warm smile of thanks, he called his executive assistant at Cress, INC. to purchase him another phone and have it couriered to the hospital.

"Thank you," he said, handing her the phone back.

Her fingers stroked the back of his hand as she took it.

"I'm going to take these to my wife now," he said.

Thankfully, the woman took the hint.

As he rode the elevator upstairs and walked down the hall, Sean hated that he couldn't play—

"Dream a little dream of me."

His steps faltered at the music filtering from Montgomery's room. Curious, he made his way to stand in the doorway. The curtain around her bed was pulled but he could tell doctors and nurses surrounded Montgomery's bed. He stepped into the room just as the curtain opened and the doctor emerged.

"Mr. Cress!" Dr. Schultz, the vascular neurologist, said with enthusiasm. "The nurse tried to call you—"

"Sean?"

The sound of Montgomery calling his name made him take a small step back in surprise before he dropped the flowers he held and rushed past the doctor to yank the curtain back. She sat up in the middle of the small bed as the nursing staff continued to remove the majority of the medical equipment. She still looked a bit weak and her eyes were glazed, but she was awake and looking at him as she gave him a loopy smile that was clearly drug-induced.

"Hey," she said, sounding a bit hoarse.

"Hey," he told her, feeling elated with relief.

He wanted to kiss her so badly but the staff prevented him from getting closer as they continued to work on her.

"Dream a little dream of me," Louis Armstrong sang.

"Mr. Cress."

He turned, hating to take his eyes off her. He listened on as the doctor explained that they had awakened her from her coma and all indications were she had suffered no major loss of brain function during the stroke. Sean felt like falling to the floor again in relief but stiffened his legs and listened to the doctor's plan for her continued recovery.

His phone arrived—already activated and programmed by his assistant—and he only stepped out of the room to call her father—who wept—and his family—who rejoiced. Sean felt a little of both.

Claiming a spot near the back wall and out of the way of the staff, he watched on closely as they worked, adjusting her bed, giving her medicine via her intravenous line and offering her slow sips of water. By the time they were done and left them alone, she had fallen asleep.

"Excuse me," he said.

One of the nurses stopped.

"The music?" he asked, unable to fight his curiosity.

"When she awakened, she was singing it," the nurse said with a smile. "So we put it on for her. We thought it was adorable."

"Wow," he said, stunned by that.

"We also let her know you've been here every day and that the baby is fine," she assured him. "Just sit tight, let her sleep and get the rest of the sedatives out of her system and then you two can catch up. Okay?"

"Okay," he said, already looking past her at Montgomery.

When they were alone, he pulled a chair close to her bed and held her hand. Never letting it go even as the nurse came in to monitor her. Not even when her father arrived to sit with her as well. And when the skies darkened with night, still he sat by her side, thankful that his family could watch over Morgan as he watched over their Montgomery.

His doubts resurfaced.

Under the haze of medicine, she had seemed pleased to see him.

But what would be her reaction once free of the medicinal drugs?

I love you, Sean.

He eyed her as his heart pounded.

Still?

He closed his eyes and when sleep came, he welcomed it.

The sound of something toppling to the floor startled him awake. Sean sat up straight and looked around at the night nurse assisting Montgomery back into the bed before raising the blankets to cover her legs.

"Anything I can get you?" the nurse asked.

"No, nothing at all," Montgomery said with only the light above the bed breaking up the darkness of the room.

Sean felt nervous as she looked at him.

"Tell me all about our baby," she softly demanded.

"It's a boy and he's such a good baby," he told her with eagerness.

"Morgan Sean Cress?" she asked.

Sean nodded. "Just the way you wanted."

She smiled in thanks.

His heart tugged at the sight of it as he filled her in on every detail he could think of about their son. Every little thing.

And her eyes were eager as she soaked it all up.

"I just want to hold him," Montgomery said. "And kiss him. And get to know him so he can get to know me."

"He'll know you," Sean assured, rising to sit beside her legs on the bed.

"How?" she asked in disbelief.

He smiled.

Her eyes dropped down to take it in.

His heart skipped a beat.

"Because you're his mother...*and* I had a shirt with your scent on it that I wrap him in under his blankets," he told her.

"You did?" she asked, reaching to cover his hand with her own.

Sean looked down at her touch. She tried to ease her hand away but he clasped it tightly. "I thought I lost you again," he said.

"Again?" Montgomery asked, shifting her eyes away.

"Those days after you—"

"Confessed to loving you?" she asked, now successfully tugging her hand away from his.

He reclaimed it, using his thumb to lightly stroke her inner wrist. "I was miserable without you. I need you—"

"No," Montgomery said, shaking her head. "Let's not do this now, Sean."

"But I—"

"My focus is getting stronger to get out of here and hold my son," she said, imploring him with earnest eyes. "Let me get home to him and have a moment to breathe after being in a coma for weeks. Then we can talk about what exactly *this* is."

"*This* is a marriage," he stressed.

"Is it?" she asked with a shake of her head as if to answer her own question.

He released her hand and his hopes. Rising from the bed, he strode over to the window to look out at the Jersey night. He was plagued with regrets over not accepting her love and returning it without question.

"Dream a little dream of me," Montgomery sang softly.

Sean looked back over his shoulder to find her lying on her side with her hands tucked under the pillows and her eyes closed as she drifted back to sleep. He lightly chuckled and smiled before turning to lean against the window with his arms crossed over his chest. When her light snores filled the air, he pushed off the glass and walked over to press a kiss to the spot just below her ear.

"I have all the time in the world, Montgomery," he told her, low in his throat, before leaving to go and pick up their son.

Two weeks later

Montgomery pressed kisses to Morgan's belly, enjoying his sleepy smiles as he wiggled his feet and hands while she attempted to put him in his sleeper. "That's Mama's baby," she cooed before picking him up to lay him against her shoulder to finish rocking him to sleep after a nice warm bath. "I love you with all of my heart. Every bit of it."

You and your father.

She could already see that Morgan would be the second coming of Sean.

Just as handsome and probably twice as charming one day.

"And some girl will love you just as much as I love your dad," she said, stroking his cheek with her finger.

"If only I could check all the boxes to be your Mr. Perfect."

At the sound of Sean's deep voice, Montgomery felt the hairs on the back of her neck stand up like she touched clothes with a static charge. With her heart suddenly pounding, she glanced over at him leaning in the open doorway looking handsome as ever in a crisp black shirt and denims.

Their eyes locked.

Love for him warmed her entire body. It was raw and pure. And so very deep.

How did I think I would ever get over him? That I ever could *get over him?*

The love she had for Sean Cress would last a lifetime—even if she remarried and moved on, she knew she would always yearn for *him*.

"I didn't know you were getting home—back. I meant, I didn't know you were getting *back* so early and he just went to sleep," she said, rising with the baby in her arms.

Sean strode into the room to stand beside her as she placed Morgan in his crib on his back. They both looked down at him. "It's okay, I'll do his night bottles," he said. "We'll catch up on our day then."

She eyed his side profile, loving the devotion for their son in his eyes.

She had sworn he would run from fatherhood, but instead he stepped into it fully. She was incredibly moved and impressed that Sean not only took care of Morgan alone, but did an excellent job at it right here in her home, earning high praise from her father and the Cress family about his insistence on doing it himself— and in keeping with what he knew she would want. Not the type of sacrifice she thought a man like Sean Cress would make. She would have bet money that he would shift the duties off onto a nanny or the like.

In the time since she returned from the hospital, she had acquiesced when he asked to remain living in Passion Grove because he wasn't ready to be away from Morgan. And apart from the addition of their child, it all felt so familiar. Hungering for him, but pretending not to.

I have all the time in the world, Montgomery.

She hadn't been in that deep of sleep when Sean whispered near her ear in the hospital. The words seemed to haunt her because she didn't want him to give up, but she feared that any newfound feelings he had were brought on by her near death and in time they would fade, leaving her heartbroken again.

She looked away when he looked at her.

"Montgomery," he said, low in his throat with hunger and pleading. "I love you."

She pressed her eyes closed, feeling the impact of his declaration surround her. And felt thrilled to imagine for a moment that he truly did. Just as deeply as she adored him.

"I love you so much," he repeated, grasping her arms to turn her to face him.

And I love you.

With all the courage she could muster, Montgomery looked up at him.

Morgan stirred in his sleep and they looked down at him until he quieted again, before Sean took Montgomery's hands in his and led her out of the room to descend the stairs to the living room. She eased her hands from his and walked over to sit on the sofa. As she stared into the unlit fireplace, she remembered the night they shared in front of it during the winter storm.

"Dream a little dream of me," she sang softly, smiling a bit as she touched her lips with her fingertips.

"Did you?" he asked, coming around the sofa to sit on the opposite end.

"Did I what?" she asked.

"Dream of me."

She eyed him before she closed her eyes as a memory from her stay in the hospital nudged itself forward.

Dream of me, Montgomery.

She stiffened.

You're the best thing that ever happened to me.

Her eyes widened a bit.

Come back to me, Montgomery. Please. I love you so much.

Those and a dozen more memories of Sean's heartfelt words to her during her coma resurfaced. She eyed him with a lick of her lips. "Because I almost died?" she asked, speaking to her newfound fears about them.

Sean looked shocked. "Montgomery, this is my love for you. No pity," he said. "I was already wrangling with my feelings for you before I got the call you went into labor."

She allowed her hope to fill her eyes. And her heart.

"You have changed me for the better, Montgomery," he said, easing a bit closer on the sofa. "I want to spend my life with you. I want to grow old with you."

Could it be?

She dropped her head and smiled when he inched over a little more.

Love me.

"I want my family. Me, you and Morgan," he said. "I know you're caught up in the idea of the perfect man—"

She shook her head. "Not anymore," she said, now inching a little closer to him on the sofa.

Sean eyed the move and smiled. Slowly.

"Someone really smart—and sexy as hell—once told my father that all men make mistakes and that no one is perfect or should expect perfection," she said, reaching to stroke the top of his hand.

We can love each other.

Sean quickly turned his hand to grip hers, tugging her over a bit as he shifted as well for them to meet in the middle. He leaned in and pressed a kiss to the base of her throat.

They *both* shivered.

This thing between us is deep. Undeniable. And lasting.

"I was wrong to expect perfection when I resented perfection being expected of me," she explained.

Sean raised his head to lock eyes with her. "Insightful," he said with commendation.

"Right?" she asked.

They leaned their faces in close, touching noses as their eyes met and held.

"My life is better with you than it could *ever* be without you," he said softly, his words breezing against her lips.

She freed her tongue as if she could catch them like snowflakes.

He chuckled at the move.

Montgomery gave him a soft smile. "You are not perfect, neither am I, but you, Mr. Sean Cress, are perfect for me," she confessed.

He captured her mouth with his own as he wrapped his arms around her body to lift her over his lap to straddle. She eased her arms around his neck as she returned his kisses and gave in to the passion.

"Let's go to bed," she said in between kisses before rising to extend her hand to him.

Sean leaned back against the sofa as he looked up at her with legs spread wide, giving off the energy that he was equipped and ready to please her. "Yours or mine?" he asked.

Montgomery tilted her head to the side with one of her brows risen. *"Ours,"* she answered definitively.

He leaned forward and wrapped his arms around her thighs, picking her up over his shoulder as he rose to his full height. She bit down on her lip to keep from squealing in delight as he carried her up the stairs and into *their* owner's suite.

Epilogue

Five months later

Montgomery bounced a plump and happy Morgan on her hip as he played with her ear as she looked out the window of the nursery at the snow falling outside. She could hardly believe it had been a year since she first discovered she was pregnant. She chuckled, remembering how freaked out they both had been by the idea of becoming parents.

And just as they thought nothing had been the same for them again.

It's all spectacularly better.

They had settled in as a family in Passion Grove with plenty of love and passion. Communication and compromise. And lots of humor—especially about her exploits as a single woman searching for a husband.

They weren't perfect. That was impossible. But they were good. No major hassles that they hadn't faced together.

Montgomery had even acquiesced on the use of a part-time nanny only during those days it wasn't feasible to take Morgan to work with her. He made plenty of use of the nursery Sean had set up for them there—another Sean surprise.

Sean limited his traveling schedule and was focused on setting up the CressTV streaming service, including securing Delphine Côté for her own cooking series. The show was just in early development and was already heavily anticipated in the foreign markets. Still, as busy as he was, Sean was home for dinner every night, and lying on his belly on the floor watching Morgan play seemed to be his favorite pastime.

Well, except for making love once Morgan was asleep in his nursery for the night.

Montgomery pressed a kiss to Morgan's soft curls that were scented with his baby shampoo. She left the nursery and walked to the home office she and Sean now shared.

"No, I'm not missing a thing about nightlife," Sean said.

"The wife has the shackles on you pretty good," a male voice said via speakerphone.

Montgomery paused.

"Yup, and I love it in every possible way you can think of," Sean said without hesitation. "My life has never been so good. But enjoy the condo. Montgomery and I are happy to have it off our hands—and turn a good profit off the sale to you."

Damn right we are.

Montgomery moved away from the door and continued down the stairs, hating to snoop. It wasn't needed. Still, it felt good to hear the partying A-list playboy rebuff his former wild lifestyle.

When she reached the living room, she settled Morgan in his playpen where he instantly bent over to gnaw on one of the attached plastic objects. She poured herself a glass of wine in the kitchen and claimed a seat on the sofa. Beside her on the end table was a photograph of her little family surrounded by her father, his new lady friend from church and the entire Cress family clan.

Family.

Perfectly imperfect.

She was enjoying the adult version of her relationship with her father who had finally admitted that he had been a fan of Sean's cooking shows for years. They both enjoyed teasing her father about that.

Her eyes landed on Nicolette in the photo.

Montgomery was still recovering from the scare of the woman's sudden fascination with Passion Grove once she discovered the small town was home to a few billionaires, celebrities and a famous writer. Nicolette was trying to talk Phillip Senior into purchasing a weekend estate there. Thankfully, her father-in-law had no interest in living in New Jersey.

Sean came down the stairs and Montgomery looked back over the sofa to eye him as he soon lay on the couch with his head in her lap. "Do you think we'll get snowed in again this year?" he asked, looking up at her.

"You know our track record for getting in jams together," she said with a naughty twinkle in her eye.

"Yeah, and now we're stuck together for life," Sean said, his eyes warm with love for her.

"And *that* is perfect," she whispered down to him before kissing her husband deeply.

* * * * *

WE HOPE YOU ENJOYED
THIS BOOK FROM

♦HARLEQUIN
DESIRE

*Luxury, scandal, desire—welcome to
the lives of the American elite.*

Be transported to the worlds of oil barons, family dynasties,
moguls and celebrities. Get ready for juicy plot twists,
delicious sensuality and intriguing scandal.

6 NEW BOOKS AVAILABLE EVERY MONTH!

#2905 THE OUTLAW'S CLAIM

Westmoreland Legacy: The Outlaws • by Brenda Jackson

Rancher Maverick Outlaw and Sapphire Bordella are friends with occasional benefits. But when Phire must marry at her father's urging, their relationship ends...until they learn she's carrying Maverick's baby. Now he'll stop at nothing to stake his claim...

#2906 CINDERELLA MASQUERADE

Texas Cattleman's Club: Ranchers and Rivals • by LaQuette

Ready to break out of her shell, Dr. Zanai James agrees to go all out for the town's masquerade ball and meets handsome rancher Jayden Lattimore. Their attraction is instantaneous, but can their connection survive meddling families bent on keeping them apart?

#2907 MARRIED BY MIDNIGHT

Dynasties: Tech Tycoons • by Shannon McKenna

Ronnie Moss is in trouble. The brilliant television host needs a last-minute husband to fulfill her family's marriage mandate before she turns thirty— at midnight. Then comes sexy stranger Wes Brody, who volunteers himself. But is this convenient arrangement too good to be true?

#2908 SNOWED IN SECRETS

Angel's Share • by Jules Bennett

After distillery owner Sara Hawthorne and Ian Ford spend one hot night together, they don't expect to see each other again...until he shows up for their scheduled interview about her family business. Now snowed in, can they keep it professional?

#2909 WHAT HAPPENS AFTER HOURS

404 Sound • by Kianna Alexander

Recording studio exec Miles Woodson needs a showstopping act for his charity talent show, and R & B superstar Cambria Harding fits the bill. But when long days working together become steamy nights, can these opposites make both their passion project and relationship work?

#2910 BAD BOY WITH BENEFITS

The Kane Heirs • by Cynthia St. Aubin

Sent to audit his distillery, Marlowe Kane should keep her distance from bad boy owner Law Renaud. But when a storm prevents her from getting home, they can't resist, and their relationship awakens a passion in both that could cost them everything...

SPECIAL EXCERPT FROM

(H) HARLEQUIN
DESIRE

*Returning to her hometown, brokenhearted journalist
Adaline Harlow is supposed to write an exposé on
Colter Ward, Texas's Sexiest Bachelor, and that
assignment does not include falling for him! As the
attraction grows, will they break their no-love-allowed
rule for a second chance at happiness?*

Read on for a sneak peek at
Most Eligible Cowboy
by USA TODAY *bestselling author Stacey Kennedy.*

"You want your story. I want these women off my back…
Stay in town and agree to being my girlfriend until this
story dies down and I'll give you the exclusive you want."

"Her eyes widened. "You're serious?"

"Deadly serious," he confirmed. "I want my life back.
You need a promotion. This is a win-win for both of us."

She gave a cute wiggle on her stool. "I think you're
giving me far too much credit. Why would women care if
I'm your girlfriend?"

"I don't think you're giving yourself enough credit."
He stared at her parted lips, shining eyes, her slowly

building smile, and closed the distance between them, waiting for her to back away. When she didn't and even leaned in closer, he said, "Trust me, they'd care." He captured her mouth, cupping her warm face, telling himself the whole damn time this was a terrible idea.

Don't miss what happens next in...
Most Eligible Cowboy
by USA TODAY *bestselling author Stacey Kennedy.*

Available November 2022 wherever
Harlequin Desire books and ebooks are sold.

Harlequin.com